PAWS AND PUZZLES

WHISKEY MYSTERY #1

In Your Face Ink LLC
9524 W. Camelback Road
#130-182
Glendale, AZ 85305
www.inyourfaceink.com

First printed in the United States of America by In Your Face Ink

ISBN 978-1-7379733-2-4 (hardback)
ISBN: 978-1-7379733-3-1 (paperback)
ISBN: 978-1-7379733-4-8 (e-book)

Book design and cover by Rick Schank of Purple Couch Creative

PIECES OF THE PUZZLE

CHAPTER ONE

At 7 a.m. Sarah Carter strolled down Main Street's grass-flanked sidewalk with her red and white Australian Cattle Dog Whiskey at her side. He was off-leash as usual and none of her neighbors seemed to care as they greeted them both with head scratches for him and "Good mornings" and "Nice days" to Sarah. It had been six years since she and Whiskey had moved to Cottageville from Seattle, where she had gone to university. But in some ways, it felt like Sarah had been here her whole life. Cottageville was where her grandmother had lived for thirty years, and Sarah and her parents had been frequent visitors, so Sarah had been adopted by the locals as one of their own.

The bald-headed grocer George, age unknown but Sarah thought was definitely over 65, was unlocking the front doors of Produce and More and called out, "Good morning, Sarah. The missus will bring Chutney by at eleven for a nail clipping."

"Thanks for the heads-up, George," Sarah said. Nail clippings didn't need appointments, but grooming did at Carter's Canine Coiffure. Sarah appreciated the forewarning of Chutney's arrival. He was a rescued Chihuahua who acted like a Tasmanian Devil with bared teeth and frenzy when it came to anyone touching his feet or when he felt threatened—and being at the groomers instantly triggered all of his fears. The last time he had come in, his razor-sharp claw scraped a bloody line up Emily's arm. Sarah couldn't afford to place her assistant in that precarious situation again. Yes, scratches and bites could be a hazard of unwanted washing and clipping, but the deep dig-in almost sent Emily to the ER.

So instead of continuing their usual morning stroll, Sarah and Whiskey detoured into the hardware store, which opened early, to buy forearm length tough leather work gloves as a precaution and a way to get the Chutney nail cutting job done. Whiskey wiggled his nose at the scents of metal, wood, and paint, and tried to sneak down the aisle containing bird seed. Sarah spied him and commanded, "Follow." He stopped, acknowledged her with eye contact, and then dropped his bushy red and white tail and flattened his ears like he was sad to disappoint her before slinking in her wake.

Sarah pulled three pairs of gloves over her pale, freckled arms before deciding which ones were best for the job and then walked to the cash register. She greeted Daniel, the offspring included on the store's outside signage: Buck and Son Hardware. The s had been removed years ago after his parents discovered Daniel would be their only child.

"Gorgeous weather," Daniel said as he ran Sarah's credit card and gave a beef jerky treat to Whiskey. Whiskey inhaled it and then crept behind the counter and pawed Daniel asking for another.

"Ignore him," Sarah said, shaking her head. "He's insatiable and lacking in manners."

Daniel laughed. "His big, sad brown eyes certainly make it seem like he's saying, 'Please, please, please.'"

"Something like that. But still, he doesn't need another." Sarah smiled and appreciated the warmth in Daniel's eyes, which were almost the same color as Whiskey's. Sarah knew that Whiskey would be given another treat when they stopped to say hi to her best friend Ginger who owned Java and Juice and that he'd get a biscuit from Bill, an elderly man who read his morning paper and drank his coffee—rain or shine—on his big wooden front porch next to a gallon-sized glass jar of dog biscuits. Every dog in the town loved to stroll through the town and stop at Bill's. And if Bill had a tail, Sarah mused, he'd wag it, as he seemed just as excited to see the dogs as they were to see him and his treat jar. He was a widower, and Sarah thought all of the visitors made him feel less lonely.

But before they could go to the end of the block and to Bill's, Sarah pushed open the painted red door on Java and Juice, which tinkled the brass bell attached to the top of the frame. Ginger's back was to the door as she was frothing foam for the top of someone's latte. Her blond curly hair was pulled into an unruly high ponytail that peeked from under a colorful abstract print scarf. Ginger kept her hair covered so it didn't interfere with the fabulous food and refreshing drinks she made and served.

A few of the regulars stood in line catching up on the latest town gossip. Sarah heard a snide comment about the elementary school principal and two women at the far table had mentioned the name of Sarah's next door neighbor Janice Jenkins before the conversation paused. The regulars greeted Whiskey and Sarah and then went back to their conversations. Sarah didn't catch what was said about Mrs. Jenkins, as the women at the table dropped their voices after Sarah's arrival.

Whiskey parked himself next to the counter and waited while Sarah eyed the daily specials. She felt the chocolate croissant calling to her like a Siren.

Sarah walked to the end of the line and waited while Ginger's employee Jared filled the orders of the customers in front of her and Whiskey, and then he greeted them with a huge grin.

"Give me five, Whiskey!" he said, reaching his hand over the counter. Whiskey popped onto his hind feet and swiped Jared's hand with his left front paw.

"That's my man!" Jared exclaimed, before throwing one of Ginger's homemade chicken bone-shaped dog treats in the air for Whiskey to catch. Whiskey's jaws snapped like a piranha and the treat vanished from sight. Then he gave Jared a cattle dog smile, black gums stretched back and upward towards his ears and just a bit of teeth.

Jared said, "He gets me every time with that smile," before his deep blue eyes met Sarah's. "And what will you have today, mi'lady?" Jared bowed from his waist in playful chivalry, and Sarah cracked up.

"The chocolate croissant, my lord, and the usual." She handed Jared her twenty-ounce reusable coffee tumbler and then held her arms out as if clenching the sides of an imaginary skirt and curtsied.

The usual was the largest black coffee, dark roast, Java and Juice served. Sarah hated sweeteners and all of the pretentious milks and flavors people added to coffee. She liked coffee simple and high octane. And hot, never cold or on ice, no matter the outside temperature. She cultivated those tastes while in the Emerald City, birthplace of Starbucks.

"Your wish is my pleasure, mi'lady." Jared turned toward the coffee machine and filled Sarah's cup and then screwed its lid tight.

Sarah grinned. Jared was attractive, if Sarah was honest with herself. He was tall, definitely over six feet, maybe six foot two or three, with naturally ginger hair, similar to hers. She figured he was maybe three or five years younger than she was, possibly twenty-five or twenty-three, and he was a huge flirt. But she didn't take him seriously. It was difficult to with all of his joking around; he reminded her of her younger brother.

Jared handed her the croissant in to-go paper.

Before Sarah and Whiskey left Java and Juice, they met Ginger at the far corner of the counter. Sarah whispered, "How was your date?" She knew Ginger didn't want anyone to know she had a first date with Daniel last night. If people knew, the news would spread like a virus and people would have opinions that neither Ginger nor Daniel wanted to hear.

"Good," Ginger whispered. "I packed a picnic and we met at Shiloh Creek."

Shiloh Creek was a forty-five-minute drive up the interstate. Sarah thought that was wise if they didn't want to be seen by their neighbors. "And?" Sarah wiggled her eyebrows at her best friend.

Ginger laughed. "It was nice. I'll tell you more over a bottle of wine. Tonight?"

"Sure," Sarah said. "We'll be home around six. I'll make us a quick supper."

"Sounds great," Ginger said. She was happy not to have to cook or bake after doing so all day at the café.

Sarah gave her a quick hug, and then she and Whiskey left. She ate and sipped coffee as they finished their walk up to Bill's and then through the town square, the park and rose gardens, and then back to the yellow Craftsman style one-story house with the white fenced yard she inherited from her grandmother.

When they returned home, Sarah showered and dressed in her sort of uniform: jeans and a t-shirt featuring something dog related. The weather determined if the shirt would be short or long sleeved. She had a dresser full of shirts in every color in the rainbow, some with cartoon dogs, dog photos, or dog-related sayings. Her favorite was her black one with "easily distracted by dogs" emblazoned in white on the chest with a big paw print. Many of the shirts were gifts from clients, friends, and family. Sometimes she'd don an apron or a lab coat (bearing cartoon dogs or fire hydrants, balls, and frisbees, of course) over her t-shirts for the messiest of grooming jobs—such as the annual chow lion cuts, poodle shears, or the St. Bernard named Sebastian that shook a lot— but most days she tackled (sometimes literally) her canine customers in a t-shirt, jeans, and tennis shoes or lug soled boots. The Coiffure's floor got very wet, so it was important her and Emily's shoes had traction.

Sarah styled her hair by putting it through an elastic once and then pulling her hair partway through again to make a messy bun. She grabbed her phone and house keys, and she and Whiskey locked the front door and walked back through the park and passed Main Street to the road that ran parallel to it, Rosewood Drive. And while, yes, there were many roses and rose bushes on Rosewood Drive, it was also home to two blocks of connected shops on the street level with apartments overhead, followed by former homes that were now businesses, starting with Carter's Canine Coiffure on the north side of the street, followed by the town's only bakery, an architectural design firm, a lawyer's office, and an Italian restaurant, before actual residences started again.

Sarah and Whiskey's walk to work took fewer than ten minutes. When they stepped foot on the big hydrant shaped doormat, Whiskey hit the door once with his paw like "let me in." Sarah unlocked the cottage's green front door and pushed it open, and Whiskey bolted through the living room converted to a waiting and drop off area into the kitchen, which had been transformed with big stainless steel bathing tubs and more spigots and sprayers than in its original single-family home design. And now, instead of counters, the space had three stainless steel tables and stands with leather loops to hold dogs' heads steady as they were being groomed.

Whiskey, the Coiffure clients' emotional support companion, embraced his role as only a super sensitive heeler was bred to do. He greeted each dog as it walked through the door with its human. He licked the ones that seemed most anxious and put a paw on the ones whose fear filled the shop. Last month Whiskey had even jumped up on the grooming table and encircled a panicking Pekinese as Emily was attempting to express its anal glands. Little Ming-Chi wanted no part of that, but Whiskey wrapped himself around her and assured her everything would be okay.

As Sarah checked the levels in the shampoo bottles to see if any needed to be refilled—she bought the stuff in bulk—and ran through the list of clients they'd see today, she mentally acknowledged that part of her business' success was owed to Whiskey and his skill with sensing the emotional needs of people and dogs alike. He was one intuitive dog.

CHAPTER TWO

Five minutes later, while she was pulling the towels from the dryer, the front door opened. Whiskey barked once, a quick yip, in greeting to one of his favorite people. Emily Colt, aged nineteen, had arrived at her place of employment. Today, her hair was two fat black and flamingo pink braids, and she had doctored her black sueded Doc Martens to match by adding pink ribbon to the laces. She had on a plain black t-shirt dress that hit two inches above her knees and she had paired it with ripped black tights. Black and hot pink eyeliner accented her eyes. Sarah loved to see what Emily appeared in each day and wished she had had the self-assuredness to stand out when she was that age.

"Good morning," Sarah said. "I love the pink."

"Thanks." Emily smiled as sweet as a piece of candy. She stashed her purse on a shelf under the counter and grabbed a black apron from a hook near the back door. She took a look over the client list and asked, "Did you divvy up the work?"

Sometimes Sarah had one of them wash the dogs while the other groomed. Other times they both worked on the same dog, especially if it was a Great Dane or a Mastiff or a size or squirminess level where four hands were more useful than two. Just as Sarah was about to reply, Daphne Smith, decked out in a daffodil print maxi dress, with her forearms glittering with gold bangles, and wearing straw hat with an almost two-foot brim, floated through the door carrying Pierre, her buff-color French bulldog. Daphne looked like she belonged on a yacht on the French Riviera though they were about as far from a sea as they could get.

"Good morning, Daphne," Sarah said, as Emily beat her to the counter.

"*Bonjour,* Pierre." Emily reached to take the dog from his human, but he pulled his head back like a turtle trying to hide in a shell.

"He's *lunatique.*" Daphne pouted.

"He doesn't look like a lunatic to me," Emily said, reaching for him again.

"*Non, lunatique.* Moody," Daphne explained, dragging out the double o's. She handed him over the counter. "His skin's too dry. He's itchy and unhappy." She pouted again.

"We'll see what we can do to help him," Sarah said. "Leave it to us."

"*Merci*," Daphne said, though everyone in town had known her since birth and knew she had never visited France except in her dreams.

As she started to close the front door behind her, Sarah said, "We'll have him ready for you at 10:30."

Daphne stopped and turned; her blue eyes were barely visible under the hat's brim. "*Merci, cherie.*"

After she was gone, Emily mused, "Maybe she's been to Quebec and got inspired..."

"Who knows." Sarah started the water and ran her hand under it making sure it wouldn't be too hot or cold for Pierre. She took Pierre from Emily and plunked him into the tub where he lifted his leg and peed, marking the territory as his.

Emily laughed. "Every time."

Next to arrive was an octagenarian and her teacup poodle for a nail trim. Gladys Rossmiller had lived with Oodle, according to Ginger, for as long as anyone could remember. Ginger swore the dog was at least as old as her twenty-nine years. Sarah had tried to persuade her that wasn't possible. The oldest dog on record was an Australian blue heeler named Blue who lived until almost thirty, but that was in the 1920s, Sarah argued. But, Ginger had insisted. She had lived her whole life knowing Gladys Rossmiller and Oodle.

Oodle the poodle moved slowly like she had arthritis in every joint. And she was cloudy eyed with cataracts, so Sarah wasn't sure how much she could see. Her fur was grey with some white mixed in, much like her companion's. Gladys and Oodle were similar in many regards, Sarah thought, including that both seemed to be perpetually happy.

"Hello, dearies," Gladys greeted. She wore a white blouse from the last century and comfortable navy pull-on pants. Her eyes sparkled as she talked. "My, you are the height of creativity, Emily." Gladys spent her career as the high school's art teacher, though her hands were too arthritic to now hold a brush and paint.

"Thank you, Mrs. Rossmiller," Emily said, while clipping Oodle's nails one by one. The dog seemed oblivious or was at least unmoved by what was happening to her feet.

Whiskey sat next to Gladys and insisted the woman pat his head. "That's a good boy," she murmured.

Whiskey tilted his head toward her and smiled.

She grinned down at him. "Such a gorgeous boy," she said. Then she pulled a ten-dollar bill and two ones from her purse just as Emily finished. "Here's for the nail trim and a little something for you, my dear girl."

"Thank you, Mrs. Rossmiller. You are very kind," Emily said. She transferred Oodle back to her mom and watched them slowly walk the few steps to the door. "Let me get that for you." Emily raced from behind the counter and opened the door for Gladys, whose hands were full with her purse and poodle.

"Thank you, dearie." She nodded her head once. "Not as fast or capable as I once was."

Emily smiled and then shut the door behind them, but it opened again before she made it back to the counter. She turned her head to find a guy she went to community college with named Taylor—black hair, pale skin, and just her type—and he was holding an iguana.

"Ummm, whatcha doing here, T?"

"Hi, Em. I heard you worked here and thought maybe you could trim Iggy's nails."

"Uh, can iguana's nails be trimmed?" As she finished asking the question, Emily whipped out her phone from the apron's pocket.

Sarah, who was towel drying Pierre after his bath and a brief skin conditioner, said, "I think it is just like bird claws or any kind of nails. Just clip the tips."

Emily pulled up a YouTube video and watched for a minute. "You couldn't do this yourself, T?"

He visibly shivered. "I didn't want to. Didn't want to chance doing it wrong and causing Iggy pain." He wrinkled his forehead and nose. "Besides, you're the expert."

Emily stood up a little taller and said, "Yeah, well, thanks." She took Iggy from Taylor and put him on the counter. She kept a hand on his back so he wouldn't try to get away.

Whiskey took that moment to position himself between Emily and Taylor and laid down with his butt and tail on Emily's boots and his paws on Taylor's tennis shoes. It was weird and Emily had no idea what he was doing. She released a big breath she didn't realize she was holding and picked up the clippers. She tried to look the iguana in his eye to let him know she was trustworthy, but she wasn't sure he understood.

"It's okay, Buddy." Taylor ran his hand down the reptile's side.

Emily picked up his right front foot and took the teensiest bit from the end of his claw. The iguana tried to pull his foot from her grasp, but she held tight. "I promise not to hurt you," she said.

She quickly went through the other four toes on that foot and then did the other feet while Taylor helped hold Iggy down. It was over in fewer than five minutes, and Taylor looked relieved.

"You rock," he said, grinning.

Whiskey sat up between them and grinned from person to person.

"Funny dog," Taylor said.

"Yeah," Emily said. "He lives with Sarah. His name is Whiskey."

"Does he do tricks?" Taylor asked. "I haven't been able to teach Iggy to do nothing."

Emily winced a little internally at his double negative. "He does all kinds of things," she said and then had Whiskey give her five and roll over and bark three times on command. "He's the smartest dog I've ever met."

"Seems like it," Taylor said. "Well, umm, how much do I owe you?"

Emily looked at Sarah for confirmation and her boss mouthed, "Ten."

Taylor paid and then looked disappointed that their time was over. He picked up Iggy and walked towards the door. "I guess I'll see you at school," he said.

"Yep. Bye," Emily answered just as he shut the door.

Sarah laughed. "He's so into you."

Emily shrugged. "Maybe—"

She was interrupted by the opening of the door again. The uniformed chief of police James Order trailed his German Shepherd Sascha through the doorway. Sascha was there for her bi-monthly bath and blow-dry. Whiskey greeted his friend by sniffing her butt, which Emily swore Sascha wiggled just for him. She tried not to laugh.

Chief James, as everyone called him, greeted both women and Whiskey and said, "I'll be back to get him at the end of the day."

"Sounds good," Sarah said. She clipped the last of Pierre's nails.

Chief James disconnected Sascha from her leash and removed her collar and let her roam the Coiffure with Whiskey. He handed the leash and collar to Emily, said, "Thank you," and then left.

Emily led Sascha to a walk-in tub at floor level and started with her shampoo while Whiskey stood outside the tub keeping them company.

All day long the front door of the Coiffure opened and closed with one townsperson and dog or another. At noon, Jared popped in with two cranberries, walnut, and chicken salads and cups of homemade tomato basil soup, compliments of Ginger. "She figured you'd be too busy to break," he said before running back through their door and down the few blocks to the café.

"Lifesaver, as usual," Sarah said, as she ran a comb through the recently dried hair of a Shih-tzu named Sprinkles before cutting her some bangs so the poor dog could see. When she finished with Sprinkles, Sarah took a five-minute break to scarf down the soup and salad, before using a flea and tick shampoo on a golden retriever whose owner refused to use the meds yet made Sarah fight the fleas too regularly. Her heart bled as she surveyed and treated the bites under the dog's coat of semi-shiny fur. And then they did four more wash and trims and two more nail clips before it was finally quitting time.

It was after five when Sarah cleaned up the shop to close,

sweeping up hair, moving towels from the washer to the dryer, and throwing the most recently used towels in the washer. She saw Sascha was curled up with Whiskey in the waiting room, content but not asleep. "Em, can you let the dogs out to pee? I forgot all about them."

"Sure thing." Emily opened the front door and called both dogs to come. They walked with her to the grass in front of the cottage, and Whiskey lifted his leg while Sascha squatted. Then all three went back inside. Emily said to Sascha, "The chief should be here soon."

Fifteen minutes later, all of the cleaning was finished, and Sarah and Emily had set everything up for tomorrow. But there was still no sign of the chief.

Sarah texted to see if he was on his way as he wasn't typically late. She waited five minutes but received no reply.

Just as she was debating whether or not to walk Sascha to the station, to the chief's house, or to take her home with Whiskey, two of the town's four police cars, sirens blaring, could be heard speeding down Main Street.

"What on earth..." Sarah mumbled.

"Last time I heard that, two cars and a big tractor had a crunch up on the county road," Emily said.

"Or when Bunky Buffalo drank too much homemade hooch and started shooting with his shotgun at things only he could see." That had been last September, and the town had just stopped talking about it. Bunky would have shot the chief and his officer when they came to arrest him, except his aim was so off and his sight was so blurry, he couldn't hit a barn-size target from fifteen feet away. Officer John Beams stun-gunned Bunky when he wouldn't drop his

Smith and Wesson.

"Man, that was crazy," Emily remarked.

"He's lucky he didn't kill anyone." The only reason Bunky wasn't charged with trying to assault police officers with a deadly weapon was because they all knew him and took pity on him for acting out because his momma had died. Still, he was looking at more than ten years in the state penitentiary, as it wasn't his first run-in with the law.

Sarah decided that the best thing to do was to see if the chief's wife was home and to leave Sascha with her. And if that wasn't an option, she'd leave a note on their front door that Sascha had gone home with her. That was one benefit of living where everyone knew everyone else.

CHAPTER THREE

Barbara Order, the chief's brassy blonde wife, opened the door before Sarah, Sascha, and Whiskey had made it to the big white farmhouse's front porch. "I forgot it was Sascha's spa day, Sarah. Forgive me." Barbara's tangerine top perfectly coordinated with her full black skirt, embroidered with tangerines, bananas, pineapples, and mangos. She had patent orange strappy sandals on her feet. And when the breeze kicked up, Sarah registered that Barbara's hair was lacquered in a way that made it immobile.

Sarah wondered if Barbara was coming from somewhere or going to a function. "I brought Sascha home because the chief didn't come get her."

"That's sweet," Barbara said. "Oh, and how much was the investment in her beauty? I know it's expensive maintaining ourselves, at least for we women." Barbara shot Sarah a smile, which showed the lipstick on her teeth.

Sarah said, "Um, you have something on your teeth, Barbara." And then told her forty bucks for the wash and dry.

"If only Sergio had prices like that." Barbara sighed. "He charges a small fortune for every touch up and trim." She turned into her house, and Sarah presumed Barbara was getting either cash or her checkbook. Sascha had entered the house with her.

Whiskey sat on the front door mat waiting patiently next to Sarah. Sarah knew firsthand about Sergio's as she had been there once, when she first got to town. She asked for highlights and a trim without checking the price. She almost choked when they were done. Yes, her hair looked fabulous, shiny and full of life, but for hundreds of dollars, it wasn't worth it to her. He acted like he was a stylist to the stars as opposed to the residents of Cottageville. Maybe her current hairdresser Jackie didn't do as precise cuts or know the latest gel techniques or how to do a Brazilian blow out—not that Sarah's curly red hair wanted any of that—but she was friendly and Sarah trusted her to keep secrets and to help her look good.

Barbara reappeared, cash in her hand. Sarah gave her Sascha's leash at the same time as Barbara handed her a fifty. "It's what I have."

Sarah almost never carried cash. "I don't have change."

"Don't be silly. Keep it as a tip. I mean you had to bring him to us and everything. James got called out."

"I heard the sirens," Sarah said.

"Anyhoo, thank you. Sascha smells so fresh again. I'm sure he's in the kitchen demanding his supper." Barbara waved at Whiskey and then shut the door on them.

"We've gotta get home," Sarah said to Whiskey. Ginger had a key to their place, but Sarah wanted to throw together a salad and put water on to boil for the spaghetti before she got there.

They walked up Main Street and crossed through the park, and instead of Whiskey walking next to her and sniffing the whole way, when they got to Mrs. Jenkins' house, he paused. He sniffed the ground more intently around her white mailbox on the wooden post at the end of her walkway. Then he followed the scent up her walkway to her front door. He parked his butt on her rubber doormat, scratched his paw at Mrs. Jenkins' metal screen door, and whined twice.

What in the world? Sarah wondered.

"Come on, Whiskey. We've got to get home."

Whiskey cocked his head to the side and rotated his ears like he was listening to something Sarah couldn't hear.

She walked up the sidewalk toward him. "Come on, Whiskey. Let's go."

But the dog wouldn't come.

As she walked up the front steps, Sarah thought she heard a thump from inside the house. Whiskey's eyes got more intense staring at the front door. He whined again.

Sarah knocked on the door. She waited for two beats and heard nothing.

She knocked again. And then she yelled, "Mrs. Jenkins, it's Sarah, from next door. Are you okay?"

The house seemed still and silent.

"Come on, Whiskey. I don't think she's there."

Whiskey hit the screen door again with his paw and released one sharp bark.

No response came from inside the house.

Sarah tried to remember when she had last seen her neighbor. Was it yesterday afternoon or the day before? She didn't see her often, but every few days their paths would cross in town or Sarah and Whiskey would see white-haired Mrs. Jenkins, often dressed with a hat and pastel tweed suit as if she were having the Queen Mum for a visit, having tea with Gladys on her porch as they walked home from work.

At that moment Ginger strolled down the sidewalk carrying a bottle of merlot. She stopped when she saw them. "Everything okay?"

"Yes," Sarah said. "Whiskey wanted to visit, but I don't think Mrs. Jenkins is home. Plus, we have a date with you."

"You absolutely do." Ginger's hair had been taken down from its messy ponytail and it hung past her shoulders in pale waves. She wore a navy, light cotton sweater over faded jeans, and low black boots.

Sarah went down the steps and walkway to meet Ginger before she realized that Whiskey wasn't with her. She turned to see him still parked on Mrs. Jenkins' porch. "Stubborn dog," she mumbled, before racing back up the walk and steps and grabbing him by the collar. "Come on, love. We can visit her tomorrow."

Whiskey let himself be moved off the porch, after digging in his claws only once.

"That's so unlike him," Ginger said, when they finally reached her.

"I know." They walked next door to Sarah's and while she unlocked the door, she noticed Whiskey was next to her, but his head was turned, his eyes watching Mrs. Jenkins' house.

"What is it, boy?" Sarah asked.

Whiskey gave a short whine before bounding through his own front door. When they entered the kitchen, he hit his bowl once with his paw to signal that he was ready for supper.

Ginger laughed. "I think he has you better trained than you have him."

"Tell me about it," Sarah said and opened a can of his favorite dog food. Tonight, he would dine on salmon, sweet potatoes, and assorted veggies in gravy.

Ginger helped herself in the drawer that housed Sarah's corkscrews, and she freed two wine goblets from the cupboard. She opened the wine and set it aside to breathe.

Sarah filled her biggest pot with water and added a pinch of salt before putting it on the stove to boil. She asked Ginger, "Can you pull out the salad stuff? I want to change into cleaner clothes and wash my face."

"Sure. Want me to heat a jar of sauce, too?"

"Only if you don't want the fresh pistachio and basil pesto I made yesterday."

"Oooo, yum. Pesto, please." Ginger grabbed it plus lettuce, a carrot, a yellow bell pepper, a stalk of celery, and some cherry tomatoes from Sarah's refrigerator, placed everything on Sarah's bamboo cutting board, and got to work chopping everything, while Whiskey inhaled his food.

Wearing black yoga pants and a hunter green sweatshirt and with her face pink from the scrubbing, Sarah returned to the kitchen and dumped refrigerated, fresh noodles into the now-boiling water. She poured two glasses of wine and handed one to Ginger. "Cheers to our friendship," she said, clinking her glass against Ginger's.

"Cheers," Ginger said before taking a healthy swallow. "The Italians do wine right. Inexpensive and it doesn't taste like swill."

Sarah laughed. "It is true that many cheap wines taste more chemical than grape."

"And give us headaches," Ginger added.

"True," Sarah said, dumping the *al dente* pasta into the colander to drain. She ran water over it to remove some of the starch and then tossed it in a big bowl with the pesto. Ginger dressed the salad with a simple vinaigrette, and they set everything on Sarah's kitchen table.

When they sat down to eat, Whiskey curled like a comma on his big rectangular memory foam dog bed in the living room, in direct line with them. He kept one eye on them so not to miss anything.

As they ate, Sarah said, "So about your date...Did you run into anyone you knew?"

"Not a soul. I brought a blanket and a bottle of *sauv blanc* and your basic meats, cheese, pickles, olives, and bread. Daniel brought a bar of dark chocolate with dried cherries for us to share."

"Oh, nice," Sarah said. "Did you tell him you preferred dark to milk?"

"Not at all." Ginger smiled.

"Was it weird going on a date with someone you've known

most of your life?"

"No. Well, I have known him, but I've never really *known* him if you get what I mean. Yes, we went to the same schools, though he was a few years ahead, but by high school ours combined with two neighboring towns so we ran in different crowds. He played football and dated Debbie all four years and then through college." Ginger stopped there, leaving the rest of the details in the air. Sarah knew the story as it had happened right after she moved to Cottageville. Daniel came home from the hardware store to find his wife, five months pregnant with their first child, unresponsive in the kitchen. She had hemorrhaged and blood was all over the floor, smeared on the cabinets like she tried to stop it and then used the cupboards to try to stand. By the time the medics had arrived, it was too late to save her.

Daniel spent the following years working through the pain before calling Ginger and asking her if she wanted to get together for a drink. Ginger had suggested the picnic at the creek so they wouldn't have the prying eyes and loose lips of the whole town.

"He's easy to talk to," Ginger said. "But I did avoid initiating a dialogue about Debbie. He eventually brought her up, said he was sure she'd want him to keep living, to find love again."

"Wow. Bringing up love on a first date. Risky," Sarah joked before taking a sip of merlot.

"It was sweet. Didn't feel like pressure. He did say asking me out was his first foray into the dating pool and that he had always thought I was attractive. So that was nice. The whole evening was just that—nice. It was comfortable and fun as we joked a little. He asked me about my time at university and the year I spent traveling after, before returning here to open Java and Juice. He seemed genuinely interested. And I asked him if he had ever wanted to do anything else besides run the hardware store."

"How'd that question go over? Did he even have a choice?" Sarah finished her plate of noodles and moved on to eating her salad.

"He said he did. But he said his plan had always been he and Debbie living their lives here, being with their family, and working in the family businesses."

"Oh, that's right," Sarah said. "I forgot Debbie was her dad's paralegal."

Ginger nodded her head. "It's nice they got what they wanted..." Ginger's voice trailed off like she was in thought.

Sarah picked up, "And it was good for you to get away before determining you wanted to make this place your home again."

"Exactly," Ginger said. "And thank you for not referencing sowing oats and all of that other nonsense."

"You are far from cliché, my friend." Sarah held up her glass to her best friend. "And if you decide you want to be with Daniel, even if just for a while, he couldn't ask for anyone kinder, smarter, and more caring than you."

"Ahh, thank you. I love you, too," Ginger said, "And every day I thank our lucky stars that you decided to land here and become my BFF."

"To us." Sarah lifted her glass again. "We are awesome."

At that, Whiskey popped up his head and barked once, either in agreement or because he wanted to be included in the "awesome" too. Ginger and Sarah weren't sure, but they laughed.

"To Whiskey," Ginger toasted. "He's one of a kind!"

"Indeed, he is," Sarah agreed.

CHAPTER FOUR

Whiskey stood next to Sarah, who was asleep on her back. He placed his nose against hers, signaling it was time for her to get up. She opened her eyes and made eye contact with Whiskey before turning her head and seeing darkness through the bedroom window. *What time was it?* She checked her phone, charging on the nightstand. Five-thirty. *Early, but not ridiculous.*

"Okay," Sarah said. "Need to go out?"

Whiskey raced from the bedroom. Sarah stretched, slipped out from under her duvet, grabbed a white Turkish cotton robe from the back of the bathroom door, and walked to the back door, pulling it open.

Whiskey raced into the fenced backyard, sniffing the grass as he went. He zigzagged back and forth before stopping at his favorite rosemary bush and lifting his leg. Mission accomplished, he returned to the house and parked himself in front of a kitchen counter on which sat the canister of dried liver dog treats. Sarah gave him one, and then asked, "Can breakfast wait until after I make coffee?"

Whiskey replied by lying down at her feet.

"Thank you," she said, then ground beans to make her first cup of the day.

While it dripped, she put a limited-ingredient kibble in Whiskey's bowl. He devoured it before her one-cup coffeemaker finished its job. "Eating so fast might give you indigestion," Sarah said.

Whiskey sighed and then returned to the back door. Sarah let him back out to take care of the rest of his business. She sipped the coffee and felt her brain kicking into gear. She gazed at Mrs. Jenkins' house as she waited for Whiskey. No lights were on, but that wasn't unusual; it was early, and Mrs. Jenkins was a self-proclaimed night owl.

After Whiskey was back inside and had put himself back to bed, Sarah showered and dressed, reviewed her client list for the day and answered some e-mail, grabbed her to-go coffee cup so it could be filled by Ginger or Jared, and then whistled by the front door. Whiskey came running, sliding on the hardwood floors and crashing against the door. He smiled like he thought it was fun.

Sarah laughed and then shooed him aside so she could open the door. As soon as it was open, he bolted to Mrs. Jenkins' mailbox and sniffed around it in a circle, up her walkway, and, just like last night, up to the porch, onto the rubber mat, and put his paw on her front door.

What in the world? Sarah mentally questioned again. *He's never acted this way.*

Sarah trailed after him, jogging up the walkway and the stairs. Whiskey's nose was to the painted wooden slats sniffing the porch. He seemed to catch the trail of something because he followed the scent until the porch ended. He put his paws up on the railing, like he was contemplating if he could jump it.

"Whiskey," Sarah whispered, not wanting to wake up Mrs. Jenkins. "Down."

Whiskey wiggled his nose again and again at a twelve-inch section of railing. In the early morning light what he was sniffing wasn't obvious. Sarah bent to look closer. Smudges of some kind were on the white railing. Sarah pulled her phone from her back pocket and turned on its flashlight to get a closer look. The railing glowed eerily in the bright white phone light. The smudges were reddish brown. Sarah sniffed them and caught just a whiff of metal. *Oh my,* she thought. *Blood.*

She used the flashlight to illuminate the porch. A few of the same-colored splatters formed a trail from the door to the porch railing.

But what did it mean? Sarah wondered. *Did Mrs. Jenkins cut herself while working in her garden?* She was an avid gardener of mostly flowers and herbs.

There was no blood on the doorknob or on the screen door, at least not that Sarah could see.

Sarah turned her attention back to the railing and looked past it to the shrubs and ground below the porch. A stick with a sheared off end poked up towards the sky in the middle of an azalea bush. The branches around it were broken, the pink petals ragged and drooping towards the roots. *Something or someone has fallen on it*, Sarah thought. She wondered if a raccoon could cause that type of damage if it fell from the roof or the porch railing.

Whiskey's nose was to the porch again, and he was on the trail of something. He sniffed and sniffed, back and forth like a bloodhound though he wasn't, and finally down the stairs and around the side of the house towards the azalea. Sarah decided to follow him, expecting him to stop at the plant. But Whiskey sniffed the plant only briefly before continuing around to the back of the house.

From the ground level, the azalea looked even more trashed than it had from the porch view. The bush was split almost in two, except for that bare center stick and the handful of broken pieces. Around those, the branches were flattened to the right or to the left. Sarah had never seen anything like it before, and she didn't think a raccoon was heavy enough for this level of damage.

Her thoughts shattered when Whiskey barked once from the back of the house. "Shh," Sarah said, still not wanting to wake Mrs. Jenkins or any of the other neighbors. She jogged around the corner of the house toward the cattle dog.

But she stopped short.

Whiskey stood on the first step up to Mrs. Jenkins' back cement stoop. He looked from Sarah to the door and back again.

The screen door hung crooked and was attached by only the top hinge. And Mrs. Jenkins' blue wooden back door was slightly ajar and had been splintered.

Something clearly wasn't right. A chill went up Sarah's spine.

She didn't know if she should call out for Mrs. Jenkins and enter the house to see what was going on or if she should stay where she was and call the police.

She stared straight ahead at the house for two beats, listening.

The birds singing their morning sun salutations were the only sound, other than Mrs. Jenkins' neighbor on the left side starting the shower, which Sarah could hear through the open bathroom window. That neighbor, thirty-four-year-old Robert Wise, started singing the old David Lee Roth song "Hot for Teacher".

On any other day hearing that Sarah would have laughed, as Robert was the high school's music teacher, but at this moment she was wound tighter than a guitar string.

Her heart slammed in her chest as she tried to see in the back windows of Mrs. Jenkins' house. The curtains were drawn at each window, so no light nor Sarah peeked in.

"Come here, boy," Sarah said to Whiskey.

He trotted to her side and stood alert, his eyes on Mrs. Jenkins' back door.

Sarah took a deep breath and then called the chief.

He answered on the second ring.

"Sorry to call you so early," Sarah said. "Whiskey and I started our morning walk, but he stopped at Mrs. Jenkins, and well, I hope I'm not overreacting, but something isn't right. There seem to be smears of blood on her front porch railing and a bit on the porch itself, and her back screen door has been ripped from the hinges and the back door looks like someone busted it open."

"I agree that doesn't sound right. Have you seen Mrs. Jenkins?"

"No."

"Did you go in?"

"No."

"Good. Don't. Stay outside and don't touch anything. I'll be there in eight minutes. On second thought, don't stay there. Go back to your house and wait for us. Since we don't know what is going on or if whoever did this is still there, it is better for you to go home and wait."

"But what if she's in there and hurt?" Sarah asked.

"We'll figure that out soon enough. I just texted the medics and one of my officers to meet me there."

And as soon as he said that Sarah heard the sirens, and it wasn't even two minutes later she heard a screech of the tires as they turned down her road. "Thank you, Chief," she said. *And thank God we have such a small town,* Sarah thought.

She disconnected, and she and Whiskey walked around to the front of the house to meet Officer Beams, who was wearing his uniform but with his black, curly hair sticking out every which way like he had forgotten to comb it in his race to get there. An ambulance pulled to a stop behind the patrol car. Walter Parks and his wife Wendy, two of the town's volunteer medics, greeted Sarah by name.

Officer Beams asked her if she had knocked on Mrs. Jenkins' door.

"Not since last night," Sarah admitted. "No answer then. When we originally got here, I thought it was too early. I was trying to keep my voice down."

Officer Beams nodded his head. "Makes sense."

Walter, balding and pushing forty, said, "But now with the

sirens everyone in the area is probably awake." He chuckled.

"True," Sarah said.

Whiskey went to sniff Walter's pant leg, and he bent to scratch the dog behind his ears. "Who's a good dog?" Walter asked.

Whiskey thumped his tail on the ground in reply.

Officer Beams ran up the front steps and pounded on the door. "Mrs. Jenkins, it's the police. Open up."

No sounds came from within the house.

Officer Beams pounded again but received no reply.

Sarah said, "The back door is open."

Officer Beams' eyes widened at that. He ran around the house, just as the chief pulled up behind the ambulance. He exited his car and said to Sarah, "You're still here?"

"I didn't have time to go home. I was on the phone with you, and they showed up and asked me some questions."

"Ah."

Whiskey started toward the chief to greet him but was interrupted when Officer Beam's baritone voice carried from the backyard. "Chief!"

"Coming! Sarah, stay right there." Chief James, with one hand pulling his gun from its holster, raced toward the back of the house. Walter and Wendy jogged after him.

"Stay," Sarah told Whiskey. They stood side by side in Mrs. Jenkins' front yard as the Parks and the chief disappeared around the back of the house.

Sarah stared at the house looking for movement or light in any of the windows. Everything seemed so still. Sarah shivered with the thought that she hoped the house was empty and that Mrs. Jenkins wasn't in there hurt or dead. But whatever was going on, something definitely wasn't right.

At that moment the sun broke through the morning clouds. Sarah glanced at her phone to check the time. She needed to get to work soon, and she hadn't had any breakfast. She debated texting Emily that she might be late, but she wasn't sure what to say.

Sarah wasn't good at waiting. She started to feel antsy and helpless. She brought her empty coffee mug to her mouth on instinct and felt disappointment when she only tasted air. Her mind whirled. *What would have happened if she hadn't drag Whiskey away last night? Was Mrs. Jenkins' back door busted then? Or did that happen after they left?* She closed her eyes and tried to envision Mrs. Jenkins' front porch last night. *Were the blood droplets there then?* Sarah hadn't noticed them. But then again, she hadn't been looking for anything suspicious.

Now that the day was brighter, she really wanted to walk back up to Mrs. Jenkins' front porch and take a closer look. But she felt certain Chief James wouldn't like that. Especially if he determined this was a crime scene.

Those two words bounced around in Sarah's brain. Was it really possible she lived next to a crime scene? And where was Mrs. Jenkins?

CHAPTER FIVE

Fifteen minutes later, Officer Beams walked like a man on a mission through the front door of Mrs. Jenkins' house. He didn't stop to look at the porch or anything on it. He beelined to Sarah and Whiskey. "The chief says you can go now, but we will need a formal statement from you later that will be typed up and you'll have to sign."

"Sure," Sarah said. "You know where to find me."

Officer Beams flashed perfectly straight paperwhite teeth at her. *Someone's been hitting the white strips too much,* Sarah thought.

"Um..." She started before leaving, unsure of how to ask what she wanted to know. "Is...um...Mrs. Jenkins in the house?"

"No." His hazel eyes gave nothing more away.

Sarah let loose a sigh and felt a weight lift that she didn't even realize was holding her down. "That's good news."

"Except we have no idea where she is," Officer Beams said. "And the place has been tr–" He stopped himself from divulging that detail.

Sarah looked down at her sneaker. "Is there blood inside like there is on the porch and railing?"

"Sarah," Officer Beams said, which caused her to look up at him and directly into his eyes. "I'm not at liberty to say. The chief has declared this an active crime scene."

"I hope Mrs. Jenkins is okay."

"We do too, and we will do everything in our power to track her down."

"I'm sure you will." Sarah scratched the top of Whiskey's head and ears. She needed something familiar and comforting right now. "I need to get to work," she said.

"I'm sure," Officer Beams said. "Like I said, the chief said you can leave and that we'll be back in touch soon."

Sarah nodded her head. "Thanks." To Whiskey she said, "Come on, boy. Let's go."

She could feel John Beams' eyes on her as she and Whiskey hurried down their street.

As they walked into town, she texted Emily that she'd be a few minutes late. Sarah's stomach growled, and after the adrenaline let-down, she needed caffeine in her empty coffee tumbler. She popped into Java and Juice and handed her cup to Jared. Instead of his usual banter, he said, "You looked stressed this morning, Sarah. Are you okay?" Then he threw a treat from behind the counter to Whiskey, who leapt a few inches in the air to catch it, his jaws snapping shut like a gator's.

Ginger, wearing adorable faded jean overalls with the legs cuffed to her ankles and a lilac-colored t-shirt, turned from the coffee machine at Jared's comment. "He's right, you know. Did you not sleep well?"

Sarah looked around the café, which was weirdly empty for eight o'clock. "Something's happened to Mrs. Jenkins," she said, her voice barely above a whisper anyway.

"Medical emergency?" Jared asked.

Sarah shook her head. She looked around the empty café again and at the door to make sure no one was entering. "Whiskey and I found blood on her porch and her back door looked jimmied."

"What the—" Ginger started.

"Exactly," Sarah said. "She wasn't there. She didn't say she was going anywhere or ask me to get her mail. But she isn't there."

"That's not good," Jared said, stating the obvious.

Ginger frowned. "I didn't see blood on her porch last night. But then again, I wasn't really close enough and didn't look."

"I was close enough, but I didn't notice it. I was too busy trying to get Whiskey to go home..." Sarah's voice trailed off as her eyes filled with tears.

Ginger came around the counter and gave Sarah a hug. "The police will find her."

"I hope so," Sarah said, and then an idea came to her. "Though maybe we should organize a search party."

"I'm in," said Jared. "We can round up people this afternoon. We can let everyone know as they come in that we are planning a search."

Ginger said, "We'd better clear that with the chief first. But I do think we may be in a better position than the police to hear the gossip in this town. Java and Juice is ripe with it."

That triggered something in Sarah. "Yesterday morning when I came to get my coffee and croissant, I heard Mrs. Jenkins' name as I was coming in the door." Sarah closed her eyes trying to picture who was sitting at the table close to the door. "Whoever it was stopped talking when I entered. They greeted me, and then when they resumed their conversation, they talked very softly, like they didn't want me to overhear."

Jared squinted for a second in thought and then spoke the names of the customers he remembered waiting on the day before. Sarah knew everyone he mentioned but none of them seemed to be the people she was trying to place.

She opened her mouth to say so as the bell at the door chimed. Whiskey left her side and ran to Barbara, who wore a bust-enhancing royal blue tank top and matching tights like she had just come from a yoga class. Whiskey sniffed her calf once and received an ear ruffle. "You smell Sascha, don't you, love?" Barbara Order asked.

Whiskey smiled showing a bit of teeth in response, which made Barbara smile back.

"People at the gym are speculating why my husband and the EMTs are near your house this morning, Sarah."

"I'm sure they are," Sarah said. She figured Barbara set them straight, if she knew anything. Barbara was never afraid to use her voice and to correct people the way nuns and teachers were wont to do, in Sarah's experience.

Ginger said, "We'd like to help search for Mrs. Jenkins...to ask our neighbors to help...if your husband is okay with that."

Barbara tilted her head to the side and eyed Ginger. "Mrs. Jenkins is missing?"

Sarah stepped in, "We're sorry. You probably haven't talked to the chief. It looks like someone broke into her house and she isn't there."

Barbara pursed her lips. "She never mentioned..." Her voice trailed off.

"No, she didn't," Sarah said, "and usually she asks me to keep an eye on things and to get her mail."

"We close by three," Jared said. "I'll text some friends and spread the word. We can start the search then." He handed Sarah her travel cup of coffee, and Ginger handed her some breakfast pastries in a bag plus two barbeque chicken salads for her and Emily's lunch. Her eyes met Sarah's during the food handoff, and Sarah understood her friend was letting her know she'd work the gossip angle. Sarah nodded her head ever so slightly in agreement.

Barbara said, "You leave James to me. I'm sure he'll appreciate our help."

Sarah wasn't so sure about that, but she stayed silent.

"Thank you," Jared said. "So, we'll all meet here at three?"

"I'll move things around so we can close early," Sarah said.

"Thank you." With that she left, and with Whiskey, she walked the couple of blocks to the Coiffure.

Emily, with her hair still pink and black, was mid-shampoo of Sergio's male Sheltie Sean, and his sister Sophia was weaving between Emily's legs. Sophia yipped once when Whiskey came through the door trailed by Sarah and ran to greet them.

And that triggered an idea. Sarah put the food on the counter and pulled out her phone. Two rings in, she heard, "Are you finally going to let me add some gold sparkle to that glorious red?"

"Good morning to you, Sergio. I'm actually calling about something unrelated to hair."

"Oh god. Are my babies okay? Did something happen?" He spoke fast and clipped like a New Yorker.

"Oh, no. Everything is great," Sarah said. She took a deep breath. "I'm asking for a favor."

Emily picked up her head and raised her eyebrows at Sarah.

Sarah smiled at her.

"I'm listening," Sergio said, though his skepticism slithered to Sarah's ear.

"If you don't already know, the police were at Mrs. Jenkins' house and they don't know where she is."

"Maybe gone to have tea with the Queen," Sergio quipped.

"I'm serious." Sarah audibly exhaled. She really didn't want to reveal too much, but she needed him to believe her. "Sergio, I was there. I found her back door had been jimmied and there was blood on her front porch."

"My god!"

Sarah was glad to have his full attention. "What I need from you is to use your chair as a therapist's couch, just like you always do. People talk to their hairdressers. Find out if she told anyone anything, like if she planned a trip or had been threatened." Sarah couldn't imagine anyone threatening her neighbor. Who would want to harm a nice old lady?

"So, you want me to probe and report gossip when people confide in me because my lips are always sealed?" Pride oozed from his last five words.

"I know they are, but we need to figure out what happened to Mrs. Jenkins. Oh, and also, if you can, spread the word that we are organizing a search party that will be launched at three this afternoon. Anyone who wants to help needs to meet at Java and Juice to be assigned to a team."

"Three p.m. Got it."

Sarah heard a blow dryer start on Sergio's end of the line. She was sure that was his signal that he was done talking to her. "Thank you," she said.

Emily caught her eye again and pointed to Sean. Sarah added, "And Sophia and Sean will be ready at noon."

"Got it," Sergio said again. "Toodle-loo."

"Wow!" Emily said as Sarah set her phone on the counter. "No wonder you were late."

Sarah chugged a third of her coffee and put a chunk of blueberry muffin in her mouth. "It's been quite a morning. And I have Whiskey to thank for most of it," Sarah admitted. "If he hadn't run off to Mrs. Jenkins' this morning, I never would have..." Her voice faded as their front door opened.

Barbara stood in the entrance with a takeaway coffee in her hand and announced, "I told James we are leading a search. He appreciated the help. See you at three." Then she shut the door behind her.

Emily wrapped Sean in a bath sheet and picked him up out of the tub and handed him off to Sarah. Sophia went into the tub next squirming the whole way. Before she started getting the dog wet, Emily said, "I can post on social media. I'm sure some of my classmates could help."

"Like the one who has an iguana?" Sarah teased.

"Maybe." Emily's eyes sparkled.

Later, when both Shelties were done and wearing colorful new bandanas, they played with Whiskey while waiting for Sergio. Emily was online chatting with friends about how to help with the search.

Sarah walked out of the bathroom when she heard Emily say, "People are so mean!"

"What?" Sarah approached and looked down at Emily's phone, which she was holding like it was something vile, like a dog turd.

"I posted on Cottageville's social media group about the search. Someone with the username NOONEYOUKNOW posted, 'Janice Jenkins is a witch. She deserves whatever she got.'"

"Who wrote that? Who is NOONEYOUKNOW?"

"I can't tell. There's no photo and a web search turned up nothing. Some of the neighbors responded, disagreeing with NOONE, who wrote a few more times. See." She pushed the phone further under Sarah's nose.

Under one posting that said, "Mrs. Jenkins is a sweet old lady," NOONE had written, "Nothing sweet about her. Under that sweet façade is a cunning and ruthless manipulator." And under the post, "You must know a different Mrs. Jenkins than our dear neighbor. We're sorry yours sounds so horrible. Ours is nothing like that" was the message, "She's the devil in tweed. Don't delude yourselves."

Sarah furrowed her brow. "I don't get it. Do you think it is just social media crap? You know, haters are gonna hate kind of thing?"

Suddenly Emily's phone made the bleep of an incoming message. She and Sarah both stared at the screen. A grainy photo had appeared in the social media messaging thread. Its color was washed out but one of the people in it was a woman in a jacket and skirt walking up the gangplank of a ship. The ship's name was barely visible. Sarah squinted her eyes. Could it be a young Mrs. Jenkins...or whatever her name was before she became a missus? Sarah wasn't sure, but she was sure that whoever NOONE was, they meant something by posting the picture.

Emily said, "While we eat lunch, can I use the laptop? I want to see if I can find information about her, like what her name was before and when that ship sailed, and why this person is so hateful."

"Of course, you can use it," Sarah said.

One of Sergio's assistants came through the door just as Sarah was reaching for a notebook. The twenty-something guy with wavy chestnut hair, clingy black t-shirt, and butt hugging designer jeans, smiled when he saw Emily. "Hey, Emily."

"Hi, Travis. Your hair looks nice." Emily faced him and smiled.

He looked down at the Shelties who circled his feet. "And

so does theirs." He scratched the tops of their heads and then patted Whiskey, too, before sliding Sergio's credit card across the counter to Emily. Emily rang up the service, while Sarah handed Travis the leashes. "Please tell Sergio that Sophia has a cracked dewclaw, but it should grow out and not cause any problems. I filed it so it wouldn't hang up on anything."

"Thanks," Travis said, signing his name with a flourish on the receipt. He hooked both dogs to their leashes and said "See you around, Emily," over his shoulder as he headed out the door.

Emily smiled after him.

Sarah grinned at the sparkle in her assistant's eyes. Then she pulled a piece of paper from a notebook and started making a list of what she knew about Mrs. Janice Jenkins. She asked Emily, "You've lived here all of your life, right?"

"Yep," Emily said, as she shoved a forkful of chicken and salad into her mouth and bent over the computer.

"Do you know how long Mrs. Jenkins has lived here?" Sarah opened her own takeaway container of barbeque chicken salad and stabbed a carrot with her fork.

"Umm, I think as long as I've been alive...but maybe not. I don't know really." Emily frowned and her brow creased. "It's like she's always been here. Like the hardware store and the town library. Know what I mean?"

"I do," Sarah said. She reached for her phone and texted Ginger: "Has Mrs. Jenkins always lived here?"

While she waited for a response, Sarah wrote: gardener, night owl, loves tea, loves hats and pastel tweedy suits. And then she stopped because what else did she know? Mrs. Jenkins seemed to like animals, or at least she liked Whiskey. She kept dried beef liver dog treats for whenever she saw him.

Sarah stabbed a bite of salad and searched her brain for more information. That's when she realized that while she and Mrs. Jenkins talked multiple times each week, it was often about the weather, gardening, the town or its people, and not much else. Sarah questioned: *How can you live next door to someone for six years and not really know them?*

She didn't know what happened to Mr. Jenkins. She didn't know where Mrs. Jenkins was from. She never heard her talk about children or grandchildren or see anyone from anywhere else come for visit. Sarah bit the end of her pen as she considered that.

Emily's fingers flew over the keyboard and every so often she'd stop and read, her finger moving horizontally across the screen along with her eyes on the words. After fifteen minutes and having mostly finished her lunch, she said, "Sarah, it looks like Mrs. Janice Jenkins appears in records about twenty years ago. Before that, I've got nothing."

"Huh? What does that mean?" Sarah filled a glass with water and drank some down.

"I don't know. It's like there's no record of her. Then all of the sudden she's in Cottageville, with an address, a phone number, and no names of relatives associated with her." Emily paused and squinted at the screen. "Including no Mr. Jenkins." She looked up and her eyes, which were wide open like an anime character's, met Sarah's.

The text from Ginger confirmed Janice Jenkins moved to

Cottageville two decades before, but from where Ginger had no idea. Town gossip said she came from Indiana or Iowa, from Vermont or Toronto, or even that she had lived for years as an American in the U.K. before buying her house in their town.

The only way to get to the bottom of all of these mysteries, Sarah realized, was to find Mrs. Jenkins and ask.

But first, they had to bathe the two terriers who had traipsed through the front door with the Presbyterian pastor's wife.

CHAPTER SIX

At a quarter to three, Sarah locked up her business for the day, and she, Emily, and Whiskey walked to Java and Juice. Sarah's heart warmed when she saw so many friends, neighbors, and sort-of strangers she recognized standing in front of the café and filling the street. Jared motioned for her to come to him, and then he helped her stand on a chair so she loomed over the crowd. The chair wobbled and Sarah felt off-balance, but she was grateful for the birds-eye view. Jared let loose an ear-piercing whistle that she didn't know he was capable of making, and this brought everyone to attention and silence.

"Hey, thank you all for interrupting your days and helping us find Janice Jenkins," he screamed from atop a chair next to Sarah. "As you may have heard Sarah and Whiskey found Mrs. Jenkins' home broken into this morning, and the police have declared her missing. Sarah, would you like to say a few words to dispel the well-meaning gossip?"

A chuckle went through the crowd. "Um, sure," Sarah said, scanning the crowd. She was surprised to see Daniel, groups of teenagers and college-age students, and even Officer Beams waiting for her to say something. "Whiskey is the one who alerted me to something not being right at Mrs. Jenkin's house." The dog let loose a sharp bark, and the crowd erupted in laughter.

"And like Jared said, we don't know much. But we do know her house was broken into and blood was on her porch." She paused and looked at John Beams who gave her a slight nod, so she assumed he was okay that she provided that fact. "And we don't know if it is hers and she's hurt. We need to find her as soon as possible. Thank you all for your help."

Jared stood tall and steady on his chair and explained how he and Ginger and Barbara, whom he called Mrs. Chief, divided the town and its surrounding lands into parcels, for up to twenty teams of people. "When you and your team get to your assigned location, if it's a field or woods, spread out a few feet from each other and walk in as straight of a line as you can."

"Yeah," Barbara piped up, "We'd hate for you to clump together and walk as one and miss something two or three feet from you." A murmur went through the crowd.

But Jared screamed over them. "The three of our phone

numbers, as well as the Chief's and Officer Beams', are at the top of your maps. If you see anything suspicious, call or text. And of course, if you find her, don't try to move her. Call emergency services immediately and then text us so we can call in the rest of the teams. We appreciate your help. Now let's go find Mrs. Jenkins."

A cheer of solidarity, like they were at a sporting event as opposed to in a situation which could mean life or death, erupted from some of the crowd. Jared stepped off the chair in one fluid motion. He helped Ginger and Barbara organize the teams and give them their papers. Emily joined her friends, and Sarah noted that both Taylor and Travis were with her. She wondered how that would play out as Emily seemed to be equally attentive to them. Sarah and Whiskey waited until the town was mobilized before asking Ginger where she wanted them to go.

"We saved your neighborhood for you. Jared will go with you," Ginger said. "Barbara and I and John will stay here and track everything."

John said, "Sarah, we searched Mrs. Jenkins' yard and the woods behind her place and yours, but you know them better than we do and may see something amiss that we missed." Hope filled his hazel eyes.

"Okay. We'll keep our eyes peeled, and Whiskey's nose to the ground." She grabbed the map from Ginger, and Whiskey craned his neck trying to sniff the paper. Sarah held it under his nose. "It's our street. See? Let's go home, Whiskey." The dog took off at a fast clip with Sarah and Jared following the white point of his tail.

Halfway down the sidewalk, Whiskey christened a hydrangea

bush as Jared said, "It's been a weird day." He and Sarah walked side by side.

"In what way?" Sarah asked.

"Well, there was the usual gossip today. People talking about the police activity at Mrs. Jenkins and the normal way things get overblown. One guy said he heard she was murdered. Another said they heard she took off to Peru. Like Mrs. Jenkins would go off to hike Manchu Picchu or do an ayahuasca journey at her age." Jared snorted.

"She is spry, but that doesn't seem likely."

"Then, just after lunch two old guys were sitting at a table having soup and sandwiches and I heard the one stage whisper to the other, 'You know, Janice Jenkins was a spy.' His buddy, a guy with hearing aids in both ears, said, 'You don't say. A spy for whom?' 'The government. An alphabet agency. I'm not quite sure.' 'I never heard that one,' hearing aid guy said. 'I was told she was rich.' 'Maybe from being a spy,' his lunch buddy said. 'I don't know. But she's supposed to be loaded.'" Jared switched between separate voices, one for each guy.

"Did they say anything else? And were they part of this search?" Sarah asked. She thought about Emily being unable to find any information prior to Mrs. Jenkins' move to Cottageville. If she worked for the CIA or something, that could be why. But Sarah said nothing aloud as she didn't want to add more speculation to what was already making the rounds.

"I didn't see those geezers in the crowd, no. After that, they switched the topic to sports, and I tuned out."

Emily nodded her head causing her ponytail to bounce like a ginger question mark. As they crossed through the park, she spoke her thoughts aloud, "If Mrs. Jenkins is wealthy, she doesn't spend it on clothing or fancy trips or anything."

"True," Jared said. "Not on her house either. It looks like all of the rest around here. Have you been inside?"

"A few times. It's filled with what you'd expect. Antiques mostly. Old lady furniture. High backed chairs with curved wooden legs and floral upholstery. Heavy, probably silk, curtains. Wool rugs in muted patterns. She has served me tea from a delicate bone china set, cups coordinated with the pot."

"Antiques and all of that stuff can be expensive," Jared said.

"Yes, or it could have been handed down, or bought at a thrift store. It would be difficult to know unless we asked her. Her clothes are probably quality, but they were also made in the last century, or at least that's how they looked. I'm not sure it matters how much money she has or doesn't." Sarah frowned.

"Not unless it has something to do with motive." He pursed his lips like he was thinking hard.

"Did you hear anything else? Any more gossip or rumors?" Sarah asked as they turned onto her street. A van from the county crime lab was parked in Mrs. Jenkins' driveway and the chief's car was still there. Sarah's heart sunk. She wondered again if she should have paid more attention last night. "Come on," she said to both Whiskey and Jared, as she entered the yard of the first house on the street. "Look for drops of blood, torn fabric, trampled things, anything."

Whiskey trotted ahead of them, his nose to the ground sniffing. Jared and Sarah walked an arm's length apart from each other with their eyes moving back and forth across the grass. "Let's go to the end of the property line and back to the street and keep going back and forth until we'd done all of the yards on both sides of the street, and then we can start on the woods."

"Sounds good," Jared said. He knelt to something in the grass, dug his finger into the dirt, and then stood back up with something shiny in the palm of his hand "A penny," he said with the enthusiasm of a pirate finding a buried treasure.

"Maybe it will bring us good luck." Sarah smiled at him, struck again by how much she enjoyed his attitude and company.

After exploring ten front and backyards, five on each side of the street, they had found nothing but a rabbit burrow, which caused Whiskey to paw the ground like a bull and to vibrate with excitement, Jared's penny, and some long-forgotten garden tools, with cracked wooden handles and rusted spades and tines. In Mrs. Jenkins' yard, they found no blood, no more shrubs or bushes or plants trampled than the one on the side of the front porch, no torn tweed, nor any large untoward footprints. But then again, the area was in a bit of a drought, so the ground wasn't primed for the leaving of prints.

As they entered the tree line behind Sarah's house, she said, "Talk through certain scenarios with me, okay?"

Jared nodded.

"So, you're Mrs. Jenkins and there's a knock at the door."

Jared immediately stopped her. "No, I don't think that's right. Not unless someone knocked at her door and she wouldn't or didn't answer. Remember, you said yourself that the back door was splintered. That means someone forced their way in."

A lump was in Sarah's throat. "It had to have happened after dark. You see the houses here. I mean we aren't on top of each other like in a city, but we can see each other. Robert next door would have seen people on Mrs. Jenkins' back stoop. Or even I may have if I had looked at the right moment. There's no cover there. No room to hide."

They stopped and stared at the back of Mrs. Jenkins' house. Even from their spot near the tree line, the screen door looked crooked. "If you're going to break in, why not go through a window?" Jared asked.

"Maybe they tried and they are all locked." Sarah wondered if the police had dusted the outside of every window for prints. She made a mental note to check for the telltale signs of powder later.

"Then that means that he or they or whomever came to the house with a crowbar."

Sarah shivered. Crimes of opportunity were one thing, but bringing tools made it premeditated. "Yes."

"Which means Mrs. Jenkins was targeted. But why? Because she was old? Of all of the people in this town, there are plenty of old, easier targets than her," Jared insisted.

"That's true." Sarah's attention went from Mrs. Jenkins' house to her dog. Whiskey sniffed the base of a tree and then ran his nose up the trunk, standing with his front paws against the tree and stretching as far as he could reach.

"What is it, boy?" Jared asked.

"Probably a raccoon crawled up there last night."

Jared circled the tree, looking up and down for a sign of claw marks. He saw none. But this tree and its neighboring three all had broken branches at the same level, like something had rubbed against them. He pointed that out to Sarah.

"Maybe," Sarah said. She examined them closer by pulling out her phone and turning on its flashlight. She looked for blood or fabric or any clue as to the source of the breakage. The leaves near those tree trunks had definitely been disturbed.

"Do you think the police did that when they did their search?"

"No way to know," Jared said. He took some photos and then turned back toward the houses to set in his mind exactly where they were, which was once again behind Sarah's house, as he could spy her back fence through the oaks.

Whiskey caught the trail of something as he darted deeper into the woods, his nose scanning back and forth what was barely a path. Sarah scampered after him with Jared close on her heels. They wound through trees and over a slight incline before heading left through brambles and scrubby brush that snagged Sarah's clothing a few times and stabbed her through her jeans.

"Ouch!" She stopped for a second to remove a one-inch thorn that had pierced her calf before stumbling on the uneven terrain after Whiskey. Jared stopped short when she did.

"That dog can really go." Jared's voice sounded breathy like he had raced the last quarter-mile.

Sarah looked over her shoulder at him. His face was flushed. His eyes were wide. "Are you okay?" she asked.

"Yes. We probably should have thought about bringing water. Who knows how long we'll be out here."

"We can always circle back to my house if we need a break," Sarah said, and then after a beat, "though I'm not even sure where we are right now." She couldn't see out of the trees.

"Me neither," Jared said, pulling his phone from his pocket and opening his map app. "Not super service, but we have some."

They walked faster to catch up to Whiskey, just as Whiskey slowed to sniff a particular stick-like plant that seemed more dead than alive with dried out leaves and the coloring of an elephant. Sarah snapped a brittle branch from its top. Whiskey was more concerned with the ground around it and the green plants to both sides. Those leaves had a sheen.

"Whiskey, get out of there," Sarah said, grabbing his collar to pull him back, trying to avoid touching the leaves.

"What's wrong?" Jared asked.

"Poison ivy," Sarah said.

Jared leaned over them for a closer look. "No, I think that's poison oak."

"Poison is poison," Sarah said. "I don't want it on him, and I don't want him bringing that onto my furniture or bed."

"Point taken," Jared said, "Come on, Whiskey. Let's go." He tried to steer the dog back on the trail, but Whiskey would not be deterred. He slipped from their grasp, dove into the bush, and wriggled around in it.

"No, Whiskey," Sarah pleaded.

"Are you allergic?" Jared asked.

"I've only gotten a rash once. Come on, Whiskey," Sarah pleaded again.

But when the dog popped out of the plant, he had something in his mouth. He turned toward Sarah and sneezed. A fragment of flannel fell to the ground.

Sarah and Jared bent at the same time to inspect it and barely avoided conking heads. "That hasn't been out here long," he said. "It's too clean. Do you know if–"

"No," Sarah interrupted. "Seems too hot for flannel."

"Yes, but older people can be chronically cold. My grandma always is."

"True." She frowned. "We don't have gloves or a plastic bag."

Jared took photos of the cloth and the surrounding area. And from his phone's GPS, he took a screenshot of the coordinates of where they were. Then he texted the chief to ask what he'd like them to do. To Sarah, he said, "Whiskey may have found a clue."

"Good boy, Whiskey," Sarah oozed, while trying to avoid touching him. He'd need a chlorhexidine bath as soon as they got back.

Chief James told them to stay right where they were, that he was on his way. Sarah commanded Whiskey to stay, too, so he curled up on a bare patch of dirt and eyed them while Sarah and Jared picked up sticks and poked around the underbrush and ivy looking for more clues.

CHAPTER SEVEN

By the time Jared and Sarah finished talking to the chief, they had walked back to Sarah's house and washed Whiskey using an outside spigot and an oil-banishing shampoo, Sarah was spent, and darkness had descended on the town. She offered Jared a drink, but he declined saying he had to be at work before the sun came up. It was almost past his bedtime.

He reached for her and pulled her into an all-encompassing hug, which caught Sarah by surprise, so she was stiffer than cardboard and didn't have time to reciprocate before he released her. "Uhh, sorry," he mumbled, his face turning pink.

"No, I'm sorry," Sarah said. "I wasn't expecting that, but it wasn't unwelcome."

"Uh, okay," Jared said. "Well, see you tomorrow."

"Yes. And thank you for all of your help today, organizing things, and searching with me and Whiskey."

"Of course." He turned and walked up the street, with a lanky grace, confidence, and ease of movement that reminded Sarah of a Great Dane in motion.

She closed her door and turned toward the kitchen and found Whiskey standing with a paw on the rim of his empty bowl signaling it was way past his supper time. As she neared him with his dog food, he shook, pelting her with microbeads of water flung from his fur. "Geez, dog," she said. "I know you hated taking a bath, especially with cold water. But you didn't seriously think I'd let you contaminate the house, did you?"

He stared at her with his big brown eyes before hitting his bowl once with his paw.

"Okay, okay. Here's your food." Sarah scooped some chicken, rice, and pumpkin into his ceramic bowl, before searching in the fridge for some food of her own. She was too exhausted to cook so she grabbed an assortment of cheeses and an apple and a pear and put them on a cutting board. She cored and chopped the fruit into eighths and sliced cheese to create open-face fruit and cheese sandwiches, which she devoured one right after the other while standing at the sink.

As Sarah chewed, her mind kept flashing with the image of Mrs. Jenkins' splintered back door. Something was off about it, but the answer to what that was seemed to be evading her like squirrels kept just out of reach from Whiskey. Over and over, she replayed in her head the morning's events and the terrain searched with Jared. *Why were the tree branches broken? Was that a clue? And why was the screen door off one of its hinges? What did that mean?*

Sarah pulled out her phone and searched for a video on how to remove what she thought was a pin in a door hinge. Didn't it take a lot of force? Wouldn't it be loud? Shouldn't she or Whiskey have heard someone doing that and splintering the door?

The questions weighed on Sarah like a mastiff on her chest. She wondered if any of the teams found anything. She hadn't heard that they had; Chief James certainly didn't disclose anything when he came to retrieve the piece of flannel.

Sarah ran through the list of people in town and considered who was closest to Mrs. Jenkins. Gladys Rossmiller had visited with her more than anyone else, at least that Sarah had noticed. Sarah texted her and asked if she and Whiskey might stop by on their morning walk. She knew Gladys was an early-riser.

Gladys responded, "Yes. Around 7? I'll have the coffee on."

"Thank you."

Sarah put away the cutting board and washed the knife before rejoining it with its family members in the wooden block on her granite counter. Sarah walked into her bedroom with Whiskey on her heels. She stripped off her clothes as Whiskey joyously rolled his dampness and scratched his back with his paws in the air all over her duvet and her bed.

Once she showered the day's grime and dander away, Sarah crawled into bed with her laptop and continued the search Emily had started earlier. Was there really no electronic footprint for Janice

Jenkins before she moved to Cottageville? Sarah wondered how she ended up there in the first place. She planned to ask Gladys if she knew.

After an hour of searching that turned up very little, Sarah finally called it a night. She brushed her teeth and took one last look toward her neighbor's dark house. "Where are you, Mrs. J?" Sarah asked the night. "And what happened?"

During the night, Sarah tossed and turned and fought a giant octopus in her dreams. The fuchsia creature chased her through murky depths, grasping and grasping at her with its too many arms. She was breathless and needed to surface for air, but she couldn't outswim the beast. It wrapped around her body, pinning her arms to her sides. She kicked, trying to free herself, and bit into its tentacle trying to get it to release its grip. She tried to scream but she couldn't catch her breath. She thrashed about with her legs. Her heart pounded in her chest. She opened her eyes.

Whiskey was standing with all four paws atop her chest and stomach and his nose pressed against hers. Her last movements came back to her. "Did I kick you? I'm sorry," she said. "Bad dream. What time is it?"

She gently pushed him off of her and encouraged him to lay down by her side. She turned her head to the clock on her nightstand. One a.m.

Sarah crawled out from under the covers and padded into the bathroom to pee and drink some water.

As she passed by her bedroom window, she noticed a light bobbing down the street. She stopped and watched as the light shone on Mrs. Jenkins' mailbox and then on her walkway. Sarah couldn't make out the details of the person holding the flashlight, as there wasn't enough moonlight and there were no streetlights on her road.

The light stopped at the bottom of Mrs. Jenkins' porch and then diverted to the side of the house. It moved at a quick clip. *Oh my,* Sarah thought, *someone is sneaking around Mrs. Jenkins' house.*

Sarah raced from the window to her nightstand and her phone, though she hated to let the flashlight movement leave her sight. She pulled her cell phone from the charging cable and scurried back to the window. She could barely see the bobbing light now. She called the police emergency number and stated her name, her address, and what she had seen. The dispatcher, whom Ginger had gone to school with, promised to send someone quickly and told Sarah not to go outside. Sarah assured her she wasn't stupid and would never confront anyone on her own.

Sarah gripped the phone in her hand as she stared out the window awaiting the arrival of the police. She heard Whiskey sigh from the bed, like he wished she was back there snuggling with him. But she wanted to keep watch even though she could no longer see the beam of the flashlight from where she was standing. She wondered if that meant the person had entered Mrs. Jenkins' house through the busted back door. She stared at the house, straining to spy a light.

The beam of headlights turning onto the street captured Sarah's attention. Two boxy cop cars slammed to a halt in front of the house. As the car doors opened, Sarah recognized Officer John Beams in the one car's dome lights and Officer Candace Grimes in the other. Grimes was the only female on the Cottageville force, and she was someone Sarah considered a friend. Sarah felt like a rubber band stretched to its limits as she was sure the officers were making their way in the dark, most likely with their guns drawn.

Sarah scanned the darkness for anything...light, movement, a sign. She slid her bedroom window open an inch to see if she could hear anything, besides the wind and the rustle of the tree leaves. In the distance, she heard what she thought was the yip of a coyote. Sarah heard Whiskey sit up on the bed and sniff the air. She glanced at him, and he sighed again before turning in a circle and kneading the covers with his feet to get them just how he wanted them. Then he plopped down on top of them and promptly went back to sleep.

Sarah turned her attention back to the window, but she still couldn't see anything. She watched and waited. At one forty-five, her phone lit with a text. Grimes wanted to know if she was still awake and if they could stop by.

"Yes," Sarah texted, and then she grabbed her robe from its hook on the bathroom door. "We're getting company," she said to Whiskey. "Be a good boy."

She walked to the front door and opened it, and Grimes and Beams stepped inside. Sarah offered to make coffee, but they declined. Whiskey ran into the room at the sound of the door opening. He greeted the guests with one staccato bark. Grimes scratched behind his ears, and Whiskey leaned into her.

"Hello, love," Grimes said to Whiskey, and to Sarah, she said, "We just want to hear from you what you saw."

Sarah repeated what she told the dispatcher as they sat in her living room, with Whiskey lying on the floor between them. She felt reassured that she had closed the curtains and blinds before turning on the light. She hated to think whoever was out there could be looking in.

"Could you tell the flashlight holder's gender?" Beams asked. He had removed his hat and placed it on his knee. His curls were once again every which way, like he had been roused from slumber to respond to the call.

"No. Not enough moonlight to see anything. In fact, if the person didn't have a flashlight guiding their way, I never would have known someone was out there."

Beams nodded his head.

"You didn't find anyone, did you?" Sarah asked.

"No," Grimes said. "I think when we pulled up, we spooked them or him or her. We found no one in the house or hiding anywhere nearby. From which direction did the light come?"

"The same way you did, I think." Sarah closed her eyes and tried to recall which house the light was in front of when she first saw it. "It was on the street, but maybe in front of Robert Wise's or between his house and Mrs. Jenkins' house when I first saw it. I was immediately suspicious, since people around here don't take after midnight strolls. And then when I saw the light travel toward and around Mrs. Jenkins' house, well–"

Grimes cut in, "That's when you called us."

"Yes." Sarah looked at Officer Beams, and asked, "Did it look any different than when you were in there yesterday morning?" She wasn't sure he'd answer, but Sarah really wanted to know. She wondered if whomever it was had been looking for something. Why else would anyone poke around a crime scene in the middle of the night?

"Not that we could tell," Beams said. He paused, like he wanted to add something to his statement.

Sarah guessed and said, "But the place already looked ransacked so it would be hard to tell?" She raised her eyebrows at him.

He nodded his head, but only once. His mouth was a cross between a straight line and a grimace.

Sarah's mind whirled and she spoke her thoughts aloud. "If you were the person or people who broke in last night and trashed the place looking for something and maybe took Mrs. Jenkins in the process, why would you return again?"

"A few reasons," Grimes said, her voice barely loud enough to hear.

Sarah looked from Grimes to Beams and back again. "I watched a lot of cop shows growing up and read Nancy Drew. The way I see it, Mrs. Jenkins may not have been home when the thugs broke in and they had a hell of a time trying to find what they wanted. The first part of that scenario seems unlikely since she didn't tell anyone she was leaving. Scenario number two, she was there and tried to fight them off and they tied her up or knocked her out or something before they searched the place. Then when they left, they took her, either because they didn't find what they wanted and hoped to apply pressure elsewhere..." Sarah frowned. "Or because she could identify them. Or in scenario three, the whole beginning is the same as scenario two, but then Mrs. Jenkins fled on her own accord after they left. But I don't know why she'd do that."

Beams said, "You have a strong investigative mind, Sarah."

"She does," Grimes agreed and grinned at her.

"Thank you. And I know you can't discuss any of this with me," Sarah said. "But did you know that there seems to be no trace of Janice Jenkins until she bought the house next door and moved to Cottageville?"

Beams' eyes widened and he ran a hand through his hair. "I had no idea."

Grimes said, "What do you mean by no trace?"

"No social media, no White Pages listing history or any other directory, no images, nothing. It's strange. Even my parents and grandmother have bigger electronic footprints."

Grimes and Beams exchanged a look that Sarah read to mean they needed to investigate that trail more.

Sarah wondered if the techs pulled fingerprints from the house and if they could be traced back to Mrs. Jenkins or whomever she might have been before she moved to Cottageville. She knew the Department of Motor Vehicles took fingerprints, and Mrs. Jenkins must have a license since she had a navy-blue Buick that she occasionally drove. But Sarah refrained from saying any of that since she figured the police knew how to do their jobs.

Beams stood and Grimes followed suit. "Thank you, Sarah, for calling us tonight. If you see anything else suspicious, don't hesitate to call again."

Sarah and Whiskey both walked them to the front door. Grimes said, "I hope you are able to get some additional sleep."

"Me too." But Sarah's mind raced wondering what the flashlight wielder was after. What could possibly be so valuable that someone would enter an active crime scene? Sarah doubted it was a neighbor with morbid curiosity. She shuddered at the thought and pulled her robe tighter around her, as she turned off the living room lights and she and Whiskey padded back down the hallway to bed.

CHAPTER EIGHT

At a quarter to seven, wearing a bit of concealer to hide the dark circles under her eyes, Sarah and Whiskey walked through town and stopped by Bill's to say hello and grab a treat.

"Anyone find Janice?" Bill asked, looking up from his newspaper. Sarah noticed he was wearing new silver framed glasses instead of his usual black framed ones.

"Not that I'm aware," Sarah said. "I like your glasses."

"Thank you. We had supper together two nights ago. I cooked for her. Made *coq au vin*." Bill smiled, causing the skin to crease around his mouth and eyes.

"I'm sure it was delicious." Sarah didn't know Mrs. Jenkins and Bill saw each other socially. She wondered if it was a date, but she didn't want to seem nosy.

"It was. Succulent and cooked to perfection. She made dark chocolate cookies studded with cherries for our dessert. She likes to bake."

Sarah smiled. "Hey, wait. Two nights ago, you said. That's the night her house was broken into. I don't mean to be impertinent, but what time did she leave your house?" But before he could answer, Sarah added, "You may have been the last person to see her."

Bill's blue-grey eyes behind his glasses widened. "I hadn't thought of that. After dinner we danced around the living room a bit to Sinatra. She left about ten, I suppose."

"Have you talked to the police?"

"No. Never occurred to me. I'll call the chief after I finish my coffee."

"Thank you," Sarah said. "It may take all of us to figure out what happened. And thank you for the treat for Whiskey. We are due at Gladys' and don't want to be late."

"Tell her I said hi." Bill grinned.

Sarah wondered if he made supper for Gladys, too. Their town had a shortage of older men so maybe Bill was the white-haired set's best bet for romance. Sarah smiled at the thought as she and Whiskey walked up to Gladys' front porch.

Oodle's high pitched bark rang out from inside the house so Sarah didn't have to knock or ring the bell.

Gladys opened the door widely, and Whiskey darted inside.

"Come in, dear."

"Good morning," Sarah said, as Gladys shut the door behind her.

Whiskey was lying on the living room floor, allowing Oodle to sniff all over him.

Gladys led Sarah to a floral chintz sofa and they perched themselves at opposite ends of it. From a carafe on the glass coffee table, Gladys poured coffee into china cups and handed one to Sarah. She motioned to the china pitcher of cream and the china sugar bowl with miniature spoon and told Sarah to help herself.

Sarah reached for a shortbread cookie on a plate instead. "Thank you. I wonder if I might ask you some questions about Janice Jenkins. I realized you might know her better than anyone, as I know you've been to her place for tea."

"Yes, Janice and I are friends," Gladys said, holding the cup in both of her arthritic and slightly gnarled hands. "We take a yoga class together in the Presbyterian church basement five times a week. In fact, that's why I'm dressed this way."

Gladys was wearing a pastel pink tracksuit over a white t-shirt.

"I didn't know either of you did yoga," Sarah said, taking a sip of coffee, which she assumed from its scent and rich color was a French Roast.

"Well, it's in a chair. You can imagine the difficulty I'd have if I had to be on a mat or make my hands go flat and support my weight. There are seven of us in the class, all women and Bill, when he shows up." Gladys leaned closer to Sarah and said, "Frankly, I think he enjoys being the only male, if you know what I mean." She smiled.

"I'm sure he does," Sarah agreed. "Did you know Janice Jenkins before she came to Cottageville?"

"No, I didn't. But we became fast friends, because, well, there are so few of us our age left in this town."

Sarah nodded and took another sip of coffee. "Do you know where she's from?"

Gladys pursed her lips in thought. "Here, there, and everywhere, I believe. She said her father was in the military, was someone important. They moved around a lot."

"And later in her life, when she was an adult?"

Gladys shook her head causing her white and grey curls to bounce. "I think she still moved around. She spent some time abroad. She didn't like to talk much about herself."

Gladys finished the coffee in her cup and poured herself more after offering a refill to Sarah. She looked introspective before she said, "Actually, I just realized that she asked a lot more questions than she provided answers or information. Or we talked about nothing much. Like Bill, the town, music or art, tea, stuff outside ourselves."

"I know exactly what you mean," Sarah said. "Our daily lives are filled with talk about not much or about the present moments." She helped herself to another cookie. "Did Janice ever talk to you about Mr. Jenkins? She never mentioned him to me."

"Only that she had spent more of her life without him than with him. I assumed that meant he died when they were young." Gladys helped herself to a cookie, and when she bit into it, joy lit up her wrinkled face. Once she swallowed the bite, she said, "These are so buttery and delicious."

"They are," Sarah agreed. "Makes it difficult to eat just one."

Whiskey suddenly let loose a snore from the floor, where Oodle was curled up against him. Sarah used her phone to take a picture of the two of them. They were so sweet. She texted the photo to Gladys so she could have her own copy.

"Do you know if Janice has any brothers or sisters?" Sarah asked.

"I don't, dear. She never mentioned any. She said she moved to Cottageville because she liked the name of our town. It reminded her of a place where she used to live abroad. I think in England or somewhere in the U.K. She browsed online and looked at houses and fell in love with hers and that's how she came to live next door to you."

"Wow." Sarah didn't know what else to say. "Did she really buy it sight unseen?" Sarah barely remembered the couple from her childhood who owned the house before Mrs. Jenkins. She thought the woman had been fair complected with her hair pulled back and looked serious and the man was thin and mostly bald like the couple in the American Gothic painting, but minus the pitchfork.

"I'm not sure if she came and saw it first before putting in the offer. She never said." Gladys paused and took another bite of her shortbread. "But, I do think she may have paid cash for the house, though I hope I'm not talking out of school." She frowned.

"Why do you say that?"

"Because I said to her, 'I can't imagine taking on a new mortgage at our age,' and she agreed with me and said she doesn't believe in debt."

"Interesting." Sarah thought, *so wherever she came from or whatever she did, Janice Jenkins must have had some money,* but she kept that thought to herself. "I really appreciate you taking the time to talk to me and for giving me coffee and cookies, Gladys. I don't want to hold you up any longer, since I know you have things to do."

"Oh, yoga isn't until nine, dear. But you are right. I should walk Oodle around the block. Neither of us would beat the hare or the tortoise, but we like to stretch our legs and visit the neighbors. Thank you for stopping by, and if I think of anything else, I'll call you."

"Thank you. I really want to find Mrs. Jenkins and know what happened."

"We all do, Sarah. We all do." Gladys rose from the sofa and led the way to her front door. Sarah snapped her fingers once and Whiskey opened his eyes, popped up, and followed her. He gave Oodle one slurp of his tongue on her face before walking out into what was turning into a sunny day.

Sarah and Whiskey's next stop was Java and Juice though Sarah was positive if she drank more coffee her teeth would vibrate. She felt that amped on caffeine. So, instead, she ordered a strawberry, banana, and spinach smoothie and asked Jared to add a shot of protein powder into it since she needed to balance the sugary breakfast she'd already ingested.

"Deviating from the norm, I see," Jared remarked. He gave Whiskey a chicken biscuit, and then he threw the fruits and protein shot into the blender and pushed a button. The bladed monster came to life and loudly pulverized the ingredients into a puree in seconds. Jared poured it into a to-go glass and handed it to her. "Anything else?"

"Coffee klatch already this morning. Two salads for lunch. Whatever you think is best today."

He rang up her total and said he'd be a minute on the salads.

The café was abuzz with activity. Most of the tables were full and Ginger had the industrial sized coffee maker, milk froth machine, and the toaster oven running at once. The toaster oven dinged and Jared stepped away from Sarah to put two warmed croissants on a plate with a pat of butter and a ramekin of house-made strawberry jam. Then he ran the plate to a man Sarah didn't know who sat alone at a bistro table by the front door.

When he returned, Jared pulled two spicy shrimp salads from the cooler and handed them to Sarah. "In good health," he said, and winked at her.

Sarah smiled as she left the café and walked the rest of the way to work with Whiskey at her heels.

Thirty minutes later, she was set up for the day with an apron on, all shampoo bottles refilled, her appointments all confirmed, and her first client, Sebastian the St. Bernard in a washing tub. Sarah had just started to hose him down making sure she got all the layers of his long-haired coat, when Emily walked through the door. Her coloring was pasty, and she was wearing an olive-green top that made her look as tired as Sarah felt.

"Morning," Sarah said.

"Thanks for not adding the good," Emily said, tying the black apron over her clothes.

"Indeed. Didn't get much sleep?"

Emily shrugged. "We searched the fields until dark and the only thing we found was a fancy gold bracelet. Then we went for food, and I guess what I ate didn't agree with me. I was sick much of the night."

"That's awful. Are you okay to work?"

Emily shrugged again.

"I can make you some tea when I'm done with Sebastian." Sarah massaged the shampoo into his fur with her fingers. The dog closed his eyes and pushed against her hands like he was enjoying the pampering.

"I'll wait. I'm not sure I could even swallow water right now."

"I hate that," Sarah said. "How did it go with Taylor and Travis? They both seem to be into you."

Emily shrugged again. "It was fine. Did you find anything? Where did you search?"

Sarah brought her up to speed on searching the neighborhood with Jared, the torn piece of flannel, and about calling the cops in the middle of the night.

"No wonder you look tired," Emily said.

"Gee, thanks." Sarah chuckled.

"You know what I mean." Emily grabbed a hose attached to a nearby spigot and helped Sarah rinse Sebastian.

"I do. I had coffee this morning with Gladys, and we stopped by and chatted with Bill this morning, I found out he may have been the last person to see Mrs. Jenkins before she disappeared."

"Really?" Emily grinned. "They getting it on?"

Sarah chuckled. "Not sure about that. But I suggested he called the chief." Sarah told her about the discussion with Gladys and when she finished, Emily said, "Don't you think it's weird that none of us know anything. I mean, she's basically Janice's local BFF, and even she doesn't know where she's from or much about her."

"I know. I'm starting to think that was intentional on Janice's part. But if so, why? What was she hiding? What didn't she want anyone to know?"

"And what does someone think is in her house?" Emily asked. "If I was going to break into a house, I'd do it in broad daylight. Dress up as a service person. Carry a clipboard and wear a polo shirt with a company logo or a name tag stitched on it. No one questions those people. Why try to be all stealth with a flashlight in the middle of the night? That seems ridiculous, like it's something out of a spy novel, but not by a well-trained spy. More like an idiot."

An idea popped into Sarah's head and flew out of her mouth. "Or by someone who couldn't get away with pretending to be someone else because everyone in town knows who they are. Think about it, if you live here and know everyone, you couldn't pretend to be the cable guy or the meter reader, if everyone knows your face and knows you are the mayor or whatever."

"OMG!" Emily yelled. "We're on to something."

CHAPTER NINE

The door to Carter's Canine Coiffure opened and Chief Order came in without his dog. "Sarah, do you have a moment?" he asked.

Sarah handed off the blow dryer to Emily so she could finish Sebastian's grooming and then she pulled open the hinged counter and stepped through it so she and the chief could talk in the waiting area. "What's up?" Sarah asked.

"Thank you for having Bill call me. I heard what happened in the wee hours. We can't tell if anything is missing. I mean, we have the photos we took after Mrs. Jenkins' house became a crime scene, but we need someone who has been in her house to tell us if anything is gone or out of place. Can you take a break and go there with me?"

"Umm, yes, sure," Sarah said. "But I'm not sure I'd know much. I've only been over a few times for tea. Maybe Gladys or Bill would be better. They were closer friends with her."

"Yes," the chief said. "But you have a keen eye and instinct. Grimes and Beams shared your thoughts."

Sarah blushed. "Thank you. Okay. I will come with you." She took off her apron and threw it on the counter. She yelled to Emily, "I'll be back in a bit."

Emily nodded her head and kept moving Sebastian's fur around to dry him.

Whiskey followed the chief and Sarah out the door, and the dog jumped into the back of the chief's patrol car as soon as he opened the door.

Sarah laughed seeing the dog behind the partition. "They'll think we're taking to you to jail, buddy."

Whiskey scratched at the plastic with his paw. And Sarah held her hand up to his paw. "We'll be there soon."

The first thing Sarah noticed when they pulled up the driveway of Mrs. Jenkins' house was that the curtains on one side of the front door had been opened. Sarah got out of the car, released Whiskey from his back seat prison, and then jogged around Mrs. Jenkins' house as if a track encircled it.

The chief and Whiskey both jogged in her wake. "What are we doing?" Chief Order asked.

"Checking the windows," Sarah explained. She stopped when they were back in front of the house. "See there." She pointed to the left set of windows. "Those curtains were closed yesterday. They all were. The whole way around the house. I know because I tried to see inside to see if she was all right."

Chief Order frowned. "Why would someone…" His voice trailed off. "It wasn't us."

"Not unless they did it early this morning when looking for the flashlight person."

The chief spoke into a radio at his shoulder and asked Beams if he and Grimes moved any part of the crime scene, anything at all, like even a curtain.

"Negative, Chief," Beams' voice came through loud and clear.

Sarah's mind tumbled trying to come up with explanations. "Maybe someone was keeping watch or wanted to be able to see headlights of an approaching car?"

"That's as good a theory as any. Let's go see what else has changed." He pulled a key from his pocket and unlocked the front door.

Whiskey pushed ahead of them through the door, nose to the ground. He took a few steps to the right and then swerved to the left, on a trail invisible to humans. He followed his nose to the stairs and sniffed, sniffed, sniffed each one as he ascended. The chief and Sarah followed as if led by the Pied Piper of Scents.

At the top of the stairs, Whiskey stuck his nose in the air and strained his neck. His nostrils flared and contracted on repeat first toward the left and then toward the right, before he planted his snout back to the carpet and blazed a trail to the room at the end of the hall. He pushed the white six panel wooden door open and raced to the queen bed.

And instead of jumping onto the bed like he did at home, Whiskey surprised both Sarah and Chief James when he crouched and crawled as best as he could under the cherry wood frame. Sarah noted that the night table drawers were opened to varying degrees as were the closet doors, with clothes and shoe boxes spilling from inside. Someone had clearly searched for something.

"What is it, boy?" Sarah asked, kneeling next to the bed. The quilt and sheets had been stripped back and were twisted, the pillows half out of their cases like someone checked possible hiding places. *But hiding places for what?* Sarah wondered. *And if you were going to hide something, wouldn't between the mattress and box spring be a better choice?* Those didn't look disturbed or at least they weren't askew.

Using his back feet as leverage, Whiskey maneuvered himself out from under the bed. When he popped his head up, Sarah and Chief James noticed something sparkly in his mouth. "Drop it," Sarah commanded and put her hand under his muzzle.

Into her palm dropped a gold and cobalt blue enameled bangle bracelet encrusted with diamonds.

"Holy cow," the chief said.

"That looks antique. See how it's hinged and has that safety chain? That's got to be worth some bucks," Sarah blurted, before thinking that by holding it she may have destroyed fingerprints or other evidence. "Oh my gosh. I'm sorry." She flattened her hand, so it sat on her palm and offered it to the chief, who picked it up with a clear plastic evidence bag.

"I wonder how it ended up under the bed." Chief James knelt and shined a flashlight under the bed to see if anything else caught his eye. Whiskey squished down next to him and licked the side of the chief's face. The chief chuckled. The only thing he saw under the bed was a few dust bunnies.

Sarah was glad the chief was so dog friendly. She returned to her earlier thought of the mattress and box springs and started lifting the corner of the bed. She had it three feet in the air, but it was heavy, and she was having problems lifting it and looking under it and the same time.

The chief stood and helped her. "Looking for more jewelry, are we?"

"Yes." Suddenly Emily's words returned to her mind. "Hey, Chief, Emily said they found a bracelet in a field when they were searching for Mrs. Jenkins. Did they turn it in? Did it look old?"

"We didn't receive one. At least none of my officers reported that." He moved to the headboard and lifted the mattress from that angle. Sarah gasped when the mattress and the box spring separated. Five rings, all shiny gold, with gems bigger than a chihuahua's paw, were lined up in a row. The first ring held a ruby, the second an emerald, the third a sapphire, the fourth an amethyst, and the fifth, what appeared to be a carved moonstone.

Why aren't these being kept in boxes? Sarah wondered. "Hang on a second," Sarah said, grabbing a pillowcase from the bed. She used it to pick up the rings, one by one, and set them on the nightstand.

"Wow!" The chief exclaimed after he put the mattress down. "Strange place to keep rings and these are beauties. Barbara would kill for something like this. Well, not literally, but you know what I mean."

"It is a strange place to store them," Sarah agreed. "But if you wanted to hide them, most people wouldn't think to look there, especially that close to the headboard and center of the bed. I guess she didn't want them to be where too much weight would be on them, either."

"That's a good point," the chief said, bagging the jewelry.

"Do you think that's what the intruders could have been looking for?"

"Who knows. I mean, they could have been junkies or thieves searching for anything to make quick cash. Maybe they targeted this house because they knew an old lady lived alone in it."

"Maybe," Sarah said, but she didn't think it was very likely. Especially now that she knew no one seemed to know much about Mrs. Jenkins. She sensed there was a bigger story.

They did a quick search under the guest room mattresses and came up with a couple of more gold bangle bracelets and two pairs of gold hoop earrings, one pair shaped like an Irish claddagh and the other thick ouroboros (or snake with its tail in its mouth). The chief bagged everything though they weren't sure it was evidence. He reasoned aloud that until the back door was fixed and Mrs. Jenkins was safely back in residence, that it seemed silly to keep valuables like this on site.

Sarah agreed and wracked her brain trying to think of other places one might hide some jewelry that wasn't in places already searched by whomever trashed the place.

When the three of them traipsed back down the stairs, Sarah was stunned by the chaos in the kitchen. All of the pots and pans had been pulled from the cabinets and dishes had been shattered like someone was in a fury. Chards were everywhere, so Sarah stopped Whiskey at the door. "Stay," she said. She crunched her way across the floor, apologizing in her head and heart to Mrs. Jenkins for crushing her china. When she got to the refrigerator, she turned and saw that the chief had stopped where Whiskey did. Both were watching her. She opened the top door to the freezer and the bottom to the refrigerator. Both refrigerator and freezer looked undisturbed, and Sarah was surprised at how organized both were.

Sarah pulled white butcher papered items from the two shelves of the freezer. Each item said in black Sharpie what was in the packaging and the date. Sarah ran her hands down each item, feeling for anomalies before setting them on the kitchen counter next to the fridge. They all felt like what the packaging said.

Sarah felt defeated. She was sure she'd find more jewelry in the freezer. It was a place she thought few people would ever look. She sighed and put the white parcels back on the shelves from which they came. She was about to give up, when the six metal ice cube trays caught her eye. They were the old school kind, with the lever that you pulled to pop the cubes from the rectangular tray.

Sarah pulled the first one out. Ice, and it was opaque and looked rather old. The second and third trays contained the same. In the fourth tray, the ice was clear and looked newer. Sarah smiled when the fifth tray came out of the freezer, and she whooped when she pulled out the sixth, causing Whiskey to bark once and the chief to ask, "What is it?"

"Rings. Twelve of them. Frozen in ice. An ideal hiding place."

"I'll say," Chief Order said. "What made you think of it?"

"So few things were undisturbed in the house that I figured

that'd be the best place to look...for whatever we were looking for." Sarah crunched across the floor and handed the ice cube trays to the chief.

"As I said, you have instinct. Did you ever want to be a cop?" The chief pulled out a big Ziplock bag from inside his jacket and dumped the twelve ice cubes into it and handed Sarah back the trays.

"Not really. But I like to use my brain." Sarah smiled at him. She refilled the trays with water and put them back into the freezer, like nothing had ever happened.

They took one last look around the living room before heading out the front door, which the chief locked again with the key. As they walked down the steps to the car, Sarah asked, "Do you think she's okay?"

"I have no idea. I don't like that we can't find her. I don't like that people have entered her house, or tried to, two nights in a row." His eyes looked strained, bloodshot and worried, as he stopped and gazed at Sarah over the top of the patrol car.

"Me neither," Sarah said, "and not just because we are right next door. I wish I knew more. More about Mrs. Jenkins. More about why someone would break in. More about what they wanted. Was it the jewelry? Was it something else? And did they take her? Did she leave on her own accord? Is she still alive?" Sarah shuddered that she voiced that aloud.

"We don't know. Any of it," Chief Order said, his voice quiet like the breeze.

"What about the blood on the porch railing? Any idea who it belongs to? Male or female?"

"Too soon to know. But the crime lab said they'd put a rush on it. Sarah, I appreciate you coming here with me today and what you found. Not sure how it fits into the case, but it's definitely something. Thank you." With that, he got into the driver's side and started the car. Sarah let Whiskey in the back again before sitting shotgun. They drove the few blocks to her business in silence.

CHAPTER TEN

When Sarah and Whiskey got back inside the Coiffure, Whiskey sniffed the air, flattened his ears, and whined like he had some past trauma from the sulfuric odor he smelled. Sarah ruffled the fur atop his head and said, "It's okay, boy." On autopilot from the past hour, she asked Emily, "Hey, Em, you said you guys found a bracelet in the field. What does it look like?"

Emily was scrubbing a schnauzer with Dawn dish soap instead of the normal shampoo.

"Skunked?" Sarah asked.

Emily nodded. "Can't you smell it in the air?"

"Yes, but my head was still at Janice Jenkins'." She put her apron back on and tied it behind her. She glanced at her bookings to see who else was coming in today.

Emily's fingers worked the detergent into the schnauzer's white chest fur where the yellow musk secretion was visible. The oil, and its active sulfide ingredient called mercaptan, was obnoxious to dissolve and remove. At least the schnauzer was cooperating, like she understood this was the only way to rid herself of the stench. Sarah empathized as she knew dogs had twenty times the scent receptors as humans...and even to humans, skunks stunk.

Emily said, "The bracelet was gold, kind of thick with a design kind of carved into it. It had a hinge."

"What did you do with it?"

"I put it on my wrist and wore it home. It made me feel fancy." Emily chuckled, but then her eyes narrowed. "Why?"

Sarah audibly exhaled and wondered how much she should say. "Do you think it looked old?" Sarah typed in the description of one of the rings she found into the search bar on her laptop to see if she could find information about it. Her eyes quickly scanned images, but none looked quite right.

"Old how? Like it had been in the field for a while?" Emily must have been satisfied with the shampoo job as she started to rinse the schnauzer as Whiskey supervised.

Sarah looked up from the computer. "No, old as in antique. Would you say what you found was a piece of modern jewelry or something from a different time period? And which field did you and the T's search?" Sarah looked back down at the screen and typed a description of another piece into the search bar. She tried to be as specific as possible, but again, what appeared didn't seem quite right. Sarah looked up again and met Emily's eyes.

"Hard to tell," Emily said. "I don't have a lot of jewelry experience, at least not with the real stuff." She grinned. "And the field was the one on the edge of town. We searched it all the way to the Buffalo place. Man, what a dump that place is, since it's been empty." Emily shuddered like the ghost of Bunky's mom had passed through her.

"Emily, where in the field did you find the bracelet? Can you remember?"

"It wasn't too far off the road. We had maybe gone in ten or twelve feet through the tall grass and stuff. The only reason I spotted it is because the afternoon sun made it sparkle in that all those weeds."

Sarah frowned. *Had the bracelet been accidentally dropped?* "Em, you may have to give that bracelet to the police. We found a lot of jewelry hidden at Mrs. Jenkins' house. We don't know if that has anything to do with the break-in or her disappearance, but it was a bit odd. Odd enough that the chief bagged what we found in case it is evidence."

Emily's brow furrowed. "Mrs. Jenkins had a lot of jewelry? Like how much? I never saw her wear more than earrings and a ring or maybe a brooch on her suit at one time."

Sarah thought back through all of the times she had seen her neighbor. In the garden, she wore no jewelry at all. When she wore her tweed suits, maybe a piece or two, Sarah couldn't remember. Even at the community New Year's Eve party, Mrs. Jenkins came dressed in a gown and only had earrings and a ring. *Why would Mrs. Jenkins have all of that jewelry and never wear it? Was she a collector? A gold and gemstones investor? Or was something more suspicious going on?* Sarah had no idea, but something didn't add up. She felt like she had back in middle school when an equation was right in front of her and she felt she should know how to tackle it, but it might as well as have been written in Sanskrit. *What was the piece she was missing? Why could she not solve the problem?*

Aloud, she said, "You're right. But we found seventeen rings and a bracelet, and most were gold and precious stones." Sarah paused, before adding her next thought. "And that's just what we found."

Emily's eyes looked intense, like a Shih-Tzu's during a thunderstorm. "That's a lot of rings. Did she have a big jewelry box or one of those jewelry armoire things?"

"I don't know," Sarah admitted. "Whiskey found the bracelet under her bed. I found others hidden between her mattress and box springs and in ice cube trays in her freezer. But that's all confidential."

"Ice on ice?" Emily quipped.

"More like rubies and sapphires. I'm not sure I saw any diamonds." Sarah admitted, but then she remembered the cobalt bracelet with the small diamonds and was about to say so but the door to the Coiffure opened, so she halted speaking.

Wearing his uniform and his hat, Officer Beams stepped into the waiting area and said, "I'm sorry to interrupt, but the chief mentioned something about Emily finding a bracelet. He asked me to follow up on that."

Sarah noticed one of his black ringlets was hanging over his eye, and her fingers itched with the urge to brush it to the side. But she resisted.

Emily said, "Uh, yeah, but I don't have it here." She kept her eyes on the dog in the wash tub like she was tad guilty about keeping it.

"I can take over for you if you want to run home and get it," Sarah suggested.

"I'll go with you," Officer Beams said. "I can drive you." He paused before continuing with, "I assume Sarah filled you in?" He raised one eyebrow at Sarah, which almost made her laugh.

"Okay. And yes, she just did. Said she and the chief found a bunch of jewelry." Emily passed the towel-wrapped schnauzer to Sarah, took off her apron, and followed Officer Beams out of the Coiffure. "Be back soon," she said over her shoulder before she shut the door behind her.

Sarah rubbed the dog with a towel before starting his blow-dry. Whiskey curled into a ball near her feet and closed his eyes for a nap.

Blow drying the dog sent Sarah into auto-pilot since she did it so often. It freed up her mind to contemplate other things, like Mrs. Jenkins and her ransacked house and the jewelry. *Were they tied together? And was there more gold and gemstones that Sarah didn't find?* Sarah wondered if Mrs. Jenkins' house had an attic like hers, and if she stored anything in it? *Had the police thought to search it? Had the intruders?* She considered that her house had a crawl space, too, but it was filled with spiders and sometimes a rodent or two, so she couldn't see Mrs. Jenkins' hiding anything down there. But one never did know. Maybe Mrs. Jenkins' wasn't squeamish about such things.

Sarah made a mental note to text the chief once she was done with the schnauzer.

Thirty minutes later, Emily returned without Officer Beams, as Sarah was snipping the nails of a Jack Russell Terrier. The dog's frenetic energy made it difficult to take the tips from his toenails. He jerked and bobbed and tried to reclaim his paw from Sarah's grasp. Whiskey had tried to assist by putting a paw up on the metal platform where Sarah worked. That was Whiskey's signal for Jack to calm himself and let her finish the job, but the terrier wasn't listening.

Emily retied her apron and said to Sarah, "So, Officer Hottie asked me if you were seeing anyone."

"What?" In her shock, Sarah almost clipped the quick, and Jack pulled his foot out of her hand.

"He was trying to be all coy and cool about it. But, well, you know. He's into you." She pushed her pink and black hair out of her eyes and wiggled her eyebrows at Sarah like she was a cartoon character. It made Sarah laugh.

"What did you tell him?"

"That you are single. What did you want me to say?" Emily put the Dawn back under the sink and threw wet towels into the washer.

"Umm. The truth, which you did. Do you really think he likes me?" Sarah frowned. She wasn't sure how she felt about that. She liked John enough, but she also was attracted to Jared. But the truth was, she hadn't really dated anyone since moving to Cottageville...and neither of the men had asked her out. Though in their defense, Sarah hadn't asked them out either, unless asking Jared in for a beverage last night counted. But she figured he thought she was making a polite gesture as opposed to a pass.

"Of course, he likes you. Why wouldn't he? Any unattached

straight man in your age group would be stupid not to consider you. It isn't like this place is filled with people, and you are cute, single, own a house and a business. You're a great catch," Emily said. "And you're nice, too. Which means something...since the world has too many bitches, and I don't mean that dog." Emily pointed to the schnauzer.

Sarah laughed. "Thank you, as both your colleague and your friend."

"Of course," Emily said, then after a beat she joked, "And now that I've said that, can I get a raise?" She chuckled.

"Soon," Sarah promised. "When do you graduate?" She finished the last couple of clippings on Jack and put the dog on the floor with Whiskey. His owner had dropped him off before grabbing lunch at the Italian restaurant nearby.

Emily was studying liberal arts and planning to transfer to a four-year school for her bachelor's degree. Sarah didn't want to lose her, but she also wanted Emily to reach her educational goals. She hoped Emily would choose an online program, but she didn't want to influence her decision, so she kept her mouth shut about it.

"A.A. in May," Emily said.

"That's soon," said Sarah.

"Yes, and I can't wait to be done. I like school, but I'm ready for a bigger challenge."

"What do you want to get your next degree in?"

"Maybe veterinary medicine?"

"Wow. That's a lot of schooling."

"Yeah. We'll see. I'm enrolled as a biology major come fall, but five or seven more years may be too much." Emily looked at her boot;

she made its toe pivot on the laminate floor.

"You can do anything you set your mind to," Sarah said. "I mean you are the best dog groomer I know, besides me." Sarah smiled. "And if you want to be a vet, I'll support you through the process."

Emily shrugged. "Animals are often better than people."

"True." Sarah preferred Whiskey's company over many of the humans she knew.

Jack's owner returned from lunch and paid Sarah for the nail clip plus left a lovely thirty-percent tip. As they awaited the arrival of a malamute, Emily asked, "How old do you think Mrs. Jenkins is?"

'Seventies, maybe eighty? Why?"

"Did you see a photo of her in the house?"

Sarah thought back to the rooms she was in today and of having tea on Mrs. Jenkins' porch and in her living room. She mentally scanned the built-in bookshelves and dressers. She didn't remember any photos of the woman...or of anyone or anything else, for that matter. "No, why?" she said aloud.

"I was thinking," Emily said. "With all of the AI and facial recognition stuff out there, maybe we could scan a photo of Mrs. Jenkins and see if it could match to something or someone. It's still weird to me that she has no online footprint before coming here. It's not right, unless she was a spook."

"A spook?" Sarah asked, though she knew darn well what one was. She just couldn't wrap her head around the idea that her sweet, tweed-wearing, tea-loving, senior citizen neighbor could have been—Sarah was sure it had to be past tense—a government agent.

"Cloak and daggers, and all that," Emily said. "Like a double agent, or even a single one. Or wait, maybe she's in witness protection." Emily grinned like her dog had just won best in show.

"Maybe," Sarah said, "But we have nothing to base any of that on. Maybe she has no electronic footprint because everything was in her husband's name. And I seem to remember some episode of *Law and Order* or some other crime-related show where someone needed to go into witness protection. They said they provided the person with a whole history and created an online one too for the assigned persona."

Emily said she wasn't buying that everything was in her husband's name. "Online she never had a husband, at least that I could find. Something is fishy," she said, as the malamute and his human walked through the door.

Malamutes were fairly clean animals, unless they rolled in something putrid. Max the malamute came in for a monthly wash and a deep brushing to prevent him from leaving clumpy remnants of himself all over his home. Max and Whiskey became instant friends. They stood shoulder to shoulder, though Whiskey's shoulder was lower than Max's, and they turned in tandem in a half circle in greeting.

Sarah beckoned Max to enter the metal tub, and he heeded her command by stepping into the space and standing at attention. "Good boy, Max," she said, giving me a freeze-dried liver treat. She turned on the water and waited a moment until it was the correct temperature before hosing him down, trying to saturate his many layers of coat.

Layers, Sarah thought. *People have layers, too, to their history, their lives, their stories, and sometimes layers of hidden truth.* She wondered what Mrs. Jenkins' truth was.

CHAPTER ELEVEN

At the end of the day when they were cleaning up, Emily brought up the photo idea and AI again. That was when Sarah remembered the whole thread with NOONE. "Can you maybe try it with that photo of the woman on the ship? The photo that was posted yesterday by that hater?"

"Oh, I didn't think of that. Good idea," Emily said. She stopped at Sarah's laptop and logged into the neighborhood site. She pulled up the photo and then downloaded it to the desktop. Then she searched for a program that had the capability she wanted and was free.

Sarah looked over her shoulder as she wanted to understand how programs like that worked. But she was interrupted when the door of the Coiffure opened and Sergio walked into the waiting area, sheltie-less. He wore straight legged black jeans and black loafers with an untucked collared shirt unbuttoned to mid-chest. The shirt's silk was patterned with blue ribbons, gold Medusa heads, and gold chain links.

"I did what you said," Sergio started, "but I feel like scum, and it's all your fault." He waved his hands around like he was trying to dissipate a stench.

Sarah met him across the counter. "And what did you learn?"

"One lady said Janice Jenkins knew so much about old art that she must have worked in a museum. A woman overhead that one and said, 'No, she worked in the National Gallery or the Tate, not just any old museum.' So, I asked, 'How do you know?' Well, she hemmed and hawed and couldn't remember. So much for a reliable source." Sergio rolled his eyes and then continued before Sarah could say anything. "A different lady said she had heard Mrs. J was old money, like from New England or D.C. and that her people go back to the Rockefellers or the Carnegies. But I don't remember seeing Jenkins on any libraries or public buildings."

Sarah didn't either, and she opened her mouth to say so, but Sergio said, "Anyhoo, things that people seem to be surer of include Bill and Mrs. J were friendly, if you get what I mean, but that's not a surprise as Bill is a friend of all of the ladies since his wife passed."

"That's what I've gathered," Sarah butted in, "and good for him, and for all of them." She smiled.

"Exactly," Sergio said. "And Daphne—oops, I didn't mean to say her name—said that Mrs. Jenkins has been helping her every Thursday afternoon in the library with her French. Apparently, Mrs.

J is fluent, and Daphne says she speaks a bunch of languages. Other than that, it's all speculation. No one claims to know where she is from, why she moved here, when her husband died, or other personal details. It's like she arrived, fully formed, in Cottageville, with no real history. Which is just weird. We all have histories. Medical histories, childhood, dating histories, educational histories, you name it." Sergio frowned and shook his head like he was trying to dislodge disappointing memories of some of his own histories.

"Thank you so much, Sergio. I know it pains you to repeat all of that, but I really appreciate you doing so. And my and Emily's lips are sealed. You were never here. We never heard anything." Sarah mimed zipping her lips and throwing away the key. "But you really are the best."

"The best stylist, that's for damn sure. Now if you'd just let me put some light near your face." He reached across the counter and picked up strands of Sarah's hair that had slipped from her ponytail.

"Not today," Sarah said. "But thank you. Thank you very much."

With his shoulders thrown back, he turned and walked to the door with an escort from Whiskey. "Toodle-loo," Sergio called over his shoulder as he left.

Sarah let Whiskey pee in front of the Coiffure and then called him back in and locked them inside. To Emily she asked, "How's it going?"

"I've created an account and uploaded the photo, but I'm still figuring out how everything works. I'm going to airdrop the photo from your computer to my phone so I can work on this when I get home. I'll let you know tomorrow if I discover anything."

"Okay, sounds good," Sarah said. "Thank you for your help and for everything today. I'm sorry you didn't get to keep the bracelet."

Emily shrugged. "It wasn't exactly mine to begin with."

"I know, but finders keepers and all that."

Emily closed the laptop and handed it to Sarah so she could put it in her bag and take it home. And then they parted after Sarah locked up.

On the walk back home through the Main Street and across the park, Whiskey sniffed and marked so many bushes and blades of grass as his territory, and Sarah trailed him lost in thought. In some ways, it seemed to be that the more the town talked, the more it was confirmed that no one knew much about Janice Jenkins, at least not about her life prior to Cottageville. Somewhere, she had to have gone to school, had a driver's license or identification card or two, or even a library card. That thought gave Sarah an idea. She called Whiskey to her and turned them around in the direction of the town library. They would be open for another thirty minutes and maybe Sarah could catch head librarian Carole Binds before she left.

The big glass doors sparkled in the late afternoon sun as Sarah and Whiskey approached the stone building. Sarah pulled the door open and entered the quiet, cavernous space. The air was slightly chilled to preserve the older books, and the scent in the air was a combination of paper, dust, must, and someone's too strong of perfume. Whiskey sneezed.

Wearing a red wrap dress and minimal jewelry, Carole looked up from a book she was scanning with a bar code reader at the desk.

She parted her red lips and smiled, and then handed the book that was now checked out to a girl of seven or eight, who hugged it to her chest like it was the most precious thing in the world. Sarah remembered those moments in childhood of checking out a new-to-her book and the excitement that another world awaited her.

After Sarah and Whiskey approached Carole's elevated area, Sarah—using a toned-down library voice—greeted her. Only service dogs were permitted in the library, but Carole had, on more than one occasion, made an exception for Whiskey. He was her favorite dog around town. Whiskey jogged around the big partition so he could bypass it and visit Carole close-up. She welcomed him with a hug and some scratches, before standing again so she could see Sarah.

"What can I do for you?" she asked. Her dark, chin length hair looked to have been recently highlighted and trimmed, the cut was so precise. Definitely the work of Sergio.

"Well," Sarah wasn't sure how to approach the topic other than to just come out with it. "I've been helping the police with the Mrs. Jenkins situation."

"I saw you kick off the search party yesterday," Carole said, nodding her head.

"Oh, I didn't see you in the crowd," Sarah admitted. "Were you assigned to a team?"

"Yes, I went with the group that searched the whole downtown area. We went through all of the shops front and back, the Dumpsters out back, the alleyways. We even looked in freezers in restaurants." Carole looked pained at the thought.

"Very thorough. Did you find anything?"

"Not that we could trace to Janice."

Sarah nodded. Keeping her voice low, she said, "I have a weird request, but could you possibly pull up Mrs. Jenkins' account and see what books or what kinds of books she checked out during the past year? I know it may not mean anything, but we're at a loss."

"We meaning you and the police?"

"Yes, and many of the people who live here, it seems. I mean, we all know Mrs. Jenkins but now we're questioning how much we really know about her." Sarah paused and let the statement hang.

Carole eyed Sarah like she was considering either that comment or the request. "I see. And you're right. We talked gardening mostly, and she had me research books on non-black teas last year."

"I heard Daphne met her here weekly to practice French."

"Yes, they met in one of the study rooms. They had a standing one-hour reservation on it."

Sarah knew the library lent rooms to community organizations, students, and anyone else who needed either a room in which to meet, a quiet place to study, or a place to work on a group project. And it was always free of charge to library card holders.

"I don't think her lending history will help much, at least not with her disappearance." Carole's fingers flew over the keyboard, and she touched a red enameled nail to the computer screen. "Gardening, gardening, gardening, Buddhist philosophy, a few cozy mysteries, a Thai cookbook was checked out twice. Oh yes, I remember she said she wanted to make a surprise for Bill." Carole smiled at the screen at the memory. "And that's about it." She turned her attention to Sarah.

"No books on jewelry or art?"

"No. Not a one. Anything else?"

Sarah frowned and thought. "Umm, did she tutor anyone else in anything that you know of? Besides Daphne, I mean."

"No. At least not formally. But by the front door is a bulletin board with a bunch of community notices. A few weeks ago, she took one of the tear sheets for a self-defense class the man from the dojo was running. She asked me if I knew him and if I thought the class would be any good. My kid studied with him years ago, in karate for kids or whatever it was called. My son loved it as it was good to teach him to focus and to get rid of his extra energy. That's what I told her. I had no idea what a self-defense class for adults would be like. But you might check with him to see if she enrolled."

"Thank you for that suggestion," Sarah said. "I appreciate it and your time."

"I hope we find her soon. And that the police catch whoever broke into her house. I'd hate to think there are people running around..." She didn't finish that thought.

"Me, too." Sarah said before calling Whiskey to return to her side of the partition. Carole gave him one last hug. "Good seeing you both. Have a great evening."

"Thank you. You too."

Sarah and Whiskey exited the library and walked three blocks to Kai's Karate and Judo. Through the plate-glass windows of the dojo Sarah could see a class of kids was in session. They were in two lines, front and back, dressed in identical white gi. Two taller kids in the back row had yellow belts, but the others all sported beginner white belts. Sarah smiled at how intense they all looked, eyes on their Sensei. She made a mental note to call later tonight to either ask Kai questions over the phone or to schedule a time to meet with him in person. They had met once or twice at a Fourth of July community-wide picnic, but Sarah didn't know him well.

Whiskey and Sarah finally made their way back through town and the park and to their street. When they reached Mrs. Jenkins' house, Sarah walked onto the property and circled the house like she had earlier today with Whiskey and the chief. All curtains were closed except that front one and someone had boarded over the back door since this morning. Sarah silently cursed the boarded over back door, as she had considered entering to make sure nothing else was amiss. Sarah assumed the boarding up was the police's doing, but she texted the chief to doublecheck. Everything else looked as it had earlier in the day. Sarah debated checking Mrs. Jenkins' mailbox and taking what she found home with her, but she knew that tampering with mail was a criminal offense, and since Mrs. Jenkins hadn't explicitly asked her to get the mail, she decided she should leave it right where it was, in the box.

Chief James responded, "Yes. We want to keep everyone and raccoons and rats out."

"I'm glad," Sarah replied. Relief sat on her shoulders like a fluffy cloud. Maybe tonight would be a break-in free night. With that pleasant thought, she let Whiskey and herself into their house and prepared their supper. She figured she had a couple of hours before she should call the dojo.

CHAPTER TWELVE

At eight-thirty, Sarah sat on the living room sofa with Whiskey stretched out next to her, and she listened to the phone ring four times before the voice mail recording came on. She decided not to leave a message for Kai and to stop by the dojo at another time. Or, on second thought, maybe Gladys knew about Mrs. Jenkins' intention to take the self-defense class. *Maybe she told her about it and they did it together, like the yoga class,* Sarah thought. She knew she always preferred it when Ginger or Candace were available to take classes and attend events with her; she didn't like doing things like that alone.

Thinking about classes caused Sarah to consider the private

French instruction Daphne was getting from Mrs. Jenkins. Sarah wondered how they started. *Did Daphne know more about Mrs. Jenkins' history than others in town?* She decided to call Daphne and find out.

"*Bonsoir,* Sarah," Daphne answered in her fake French accent.

"*Bonsoir,* Daphne," Sarah replied. "I heard today that you were taking French lessons from Janice Jenkins." She paused.

"*Oui, pour six mois.*"

Sarah was happy to remember her high school French. "Six months is quite a while. Did you meet every week?"

"*Oui.*"

"Wow. I've lived next to Mrs. Jenkins for six years and I had no idea she was fluent in French."

"She is. She lived in Cote d'Azur and in Paris as a girl."

Sarah was silently grateful Daphne started speaking English. "Really? I heard her dad was in the military and they moved around a lot."

"*Non.* Well, maybe some. I don't know what her father did. But she told me she learned French as a child, while living in the country. That's when she offered to tutor me so I could become fluent."

"How nice of her. Does she tutor anyone else in French?"

"In this town? No one here seems to care about things like that." Disgust permeated her words.

Sarah could only imagine how the community had made fun of Daphne over the years both behind her back and to her face. Though granted, she could be a spectacle and brought some of it on herself. But in that moment, Sarah felt sad for her.

"Did you want to take French lessons?" Daphne asked.

"I don't know. I've never thought about it. I mean, I had four years in high school and a year of French in college. But I'm not sure how much I remember, and I rarely use it."

"I could converse with you so you could practice."

"That's sweet of you. I'd like that." Sarah meant those words. She sensed that Daphne didn't have a lot of local friends. Maybe they could better their French together...if they could find Mrs. Jenkins. "Hey, Daphne, Mrs. Jenkins didn't mention to you that she was enrolling in self-defense classes, did she?"

"Yes, she had that flyer from the bulletin board at the library. It was Kai's class. You know him, right?"

"Yes, I've met him. Did she take the course, do you know?"

"Not yet. I think it was supposed to start this week. She asked if I wanted to do it with her, but well, that's not exactly my thing."

"I can understand that. Understanding how to keep ourselves safe is important, though of course, it's a skill we hope to never have to use." Sarah envisioned Daphne removing her shoe to smack someone with her stiletto if she were under assault. That seemed more her style.

"Do you know why Mrs. Jenkins was interested in the class? I mean, did she mention any threats or feeling unsafe?"

"*Non.* She said she was old and had taken a course years ago and wanted a refresher. That was all. I think seeing the flyer was what made her think of it. We had talked about other things we saw on the board, like the grass cutting services, the tree trimming company, and the lost dog notice, things like that."

Sarah nodded her head though she knew Daphne couldn't see

her. "I just wish we knew what happened to her and who broke into her house."

"Me, too. I'm going to go to the library tomorrow for tutoring and pray she shows up, you know, like nothing ever happened." Daphne's voice sounded wheezy like a choke collar was squeezing the air out of her. Sarah was sure she was fighting back a sob.

"I would love for that to happen, too, Daphne. Thank you for talking to me tonight. Give Pierre some kisses from me."

"I will. He's such a good boy. *Bonne nuit*, Sarah."

Sarah disconnected, ran her hands through Whiskey's thick, soft fur, and let herself feel a mix of emotions. Frustration at not knowing where Mrs. Jenkins was and if she was okay. Worry that this happened right next door. Grateful that people have been willing to talk to her, and that she had friends she could rely on. And a bit of fear at being unsure this was a specific incident and not an uptick in crime in Cottageville.

Whiskey started to snore and that made Sarah's heart swell with love. She couldn't imagine her life without him, her outgoing, affectionate, protective boy.

"Come on, Whiskey. We should get ready for bed."

He plopped down from the sofa and did a full-body stretch before standing at the back door and pawing at it. She let him out to do his business, and then he followed her down the hallway to their bedroom. Sarah washed her face and put on her dog paw print patterned lounge pants and tank top with one big paw print on the chest. She brushed through her hair a few times and then crawled into bed with a book. She read for thirty minutes, but her mind kept wandering like it was trying to track down something in the periphery of her subconscious. *Was it something someone said today? Was it something I saw or expected to see but didn't?* Sarah started from when she first awoke and mentally walked through the entire day, every place she had been, every conversation she had, everything she remembered seeing or hearing. *Wait, what had Sergio said, something about the Rockefellers and the Carnegies.*

Sarah padded back down the hallway to her living room and grabbed her laptop and carried it back to her bed. She opened it and entered "old money Jenkins family" into the search engine. The only Jenkins family that appeared were the billionaires who owned a grocery store chain. They weren't old enough money, unless Mrs. Jenkins married into the family. Sarah wished she knew what Janice's prior last name was. Then again, she reminded herself, they weren't even sure she was an actual missus since there was no public record of her marriage. *Hmmm.* That still didn't sit right with Sarah. *Why would someone claim to be a missus if they weren't?*

Sarah pulled up what public record information there was on Janice Jenkins in Cottageville. It had her turning eighty at the end of the year. Her address was correct, as was her phone number. Sarah double checked that against what was saved in her contacts. But no prior addresses were listed. No husband, living or dead. No children. No siblings. No known relatives. *Was she really all alone in the world? Or did it just need to look that way? Was it possible her records had been scrubbed?*

Sarah used a search engine to see if that was even possible. She found websites talking about removing juvenile offenses from records and asking courts to conceal certain things, but nothing about removing an entire identity—or most of it—from the world wide web, which in Sarah's mind sometimes seemed more like the Big Bad Wolf coming to get a person, with all of its scams, phishing schemes, and the dark web.

Sarah realized if she kept ruminating on Mrs. Jenkins, she'd spend another night getting not enough sleep. So, she shut down her laptop and moved it to the dresser, turned out her bedside lamp, crawled under the covers, and shut her eyes.

She awoke to her phone ringing at five o'clock. She glanced at the screen before saying, "Good morning, Robert." It was Robert Wise, who lived on the other side of Mrs. Jenkins.

"Sarah, have you seen it?"

"Seen what, Robert? I'm just getting out of bed."

"Look out your window toward my house."

Sarah raced to the window and looked outside. She could see Robert standing in front of Mrs. Jenkin's house. He wore a robe over plaid pajama pants and slippers. In shaky black spray paint were the words "LIAR" on the side of Mrs. Jenkins' house. "I assume there's paint on your side too?"

"Yes. And on the front door. 'Liar, thief, bitch' the three sides say. And then a skull and cross bones was painted on that piece of plywood that covers the back door."

"Holy crap! Did you call the police?"

Just as Sarah asked that she saw the police cruiser headlights turn onto their street. She grabbed her robe off the hook on the back of the bathroom door, and said, "I'm coming outside."

When she opened the front door, Whiskey ran straight toward Robert and Officer Candace Grimes, who both greeted him.

"Never a dull moment in your neighborhood," Grimes said. "At least not lately."

"Seriously," Sarah said. "Did you hear anything last night, Robert?"

Grimes told them to stay right there, and she walked around the house slowly, taking it all in.

A second police car pulled to a stop next to them, followed by a third. The chief and Beams got out of their cars. Beams carried an SLR camera and a spotlight, which he handed to the chief. They set up to take the photos of the place, and Whiskey decided he'd supervise what they were doing by sitting next to the chief. He clearly understood who was alpha dog in this situation. Grimes mentioned the four areas of paint, and also a fifth one that Robert had missed. Someone had crudely painted a fist with an upright middle finger on Mrs. Jenkins' door mat.

"Classy," Robert said, rubbing his triceps through his robe, like he was suddenly chilled. "Do you think it could be kids, you know, thinking it's a joke?"

Grimes said, "It's certainly something we have to consider."

"Or it could be NOONE," Sarah remarked.

Grimes' eyes narrowed and she squinted at Sarah like she had lost her mind. "It was definitely someone or even someones."

"No, NOONE. N-O-O-N-E written as one word, all in caps. That's who posted nasty, hateful things on the neighborhood message board about Mrs. Jenkins. Let me think, NOONE called her manipulative and cunning and a witch. Actually, I think the username was NOONEYOUKNOW, which made me think maybe it was someone we knew." Sarah was proud of herself for remembering the words used both in reference to Mrs. Jenkins and the full username.

"Wow," Robert said. "That's hateful."

"Yep," Sarah agreed.

"When was that posted?" Grimes had pulled out a notebook and wrote in it.

"The day Mrs. Jenkins disappeared. Emily had posted about the search and invited Cottageville to join. That's when NOONE wrote those things. Some of the neighbors tried to tell NOONE that they weren't talking about the same person. That our Mrs. Jenkins was sweet and kind. But NOONE mentioned the tweed suits she liked to wear so that made me think it was someone we knew." Sarah paused. "Oh, and NOONE posted a picture, without a caption."

"A picture of what?" Grimes asked.

"It was a woman in her late teens or early twenties, in a dress, on a ship like Queen Mary or Queen Elizabeth."

"Was it a young Mrs. Jenkins?" Robert asked.

"No idea. The name of the ship or part of its name was in the photo. Emily said she was going to research that, but with everything that happened yesterday, I forgot to ask about it."

"Understandable," Grimes said. "It's been a crazy couple of days." She turned to Robert. "Thank you for calling us about this. Did you hear anything during the night? Either of you?"

"No. I wish I did," Robert said, eying the words on the front door.

"I didn't and Whiskey didn't either, or at least he didn't wake me up."

"Spray paint isn't very loud," Grimes said. "Maybe we'll get lucky and find out Daniel sold someone a can of black paint or enamel yesterday."

"We can only hope," Sarah said.

"Thank you both for your time. We'll take it from here."

Sarah called for Whiskey and he ran towards her and then past her as he headed to his house. "Thank you for phoning me," she said to Robert as he made his way to his front yard.

"Of course," he replied. "Have a good day."

As soon as Sarah entered her house and locked the door behind her, she measured out the coffee, added the water, and turned on the maker. Caffeine was one way to ensure her day would be good.

CHAPTER THIRTEEN

B y the time Sarah and Whiskey were taking their walk, word had gotten around town about the spray painting at Mrs. Jenkins. Bill called them before they had reached his house. "Sarah, can you come up here to the porch for a minute?"

"Sure, Bill."

Whiskey sat at attention in front of Bill's chair and thumped his tail in expectation of the biscuit Bill was fishing from the jar. "I heard about the activity at Janice's house. How bad is it?"

"Rude, but nothing that a few coats of paint can't cover."

Bill nodded his head. "Do you know if the police have any leads?"

"Possibly. And of course, they will check to see if the hardware store sold the paint."

"Makes sense. How long do you think the house has to stay as is?"

"I don't know, Bill." Sarah wondered why he had asked that.

But his next sentence told her. "I want to send someone over there to sand and repaint. I'd hate for her to see the place like that."

"That's sweet of you. But only the chief would know when they will be done. You'd have to get his approval."

"Of course." Bill's eyes sparkled as if helping people lit him from within.

Sarah's heart warmed. "Bill, it is super sweet of you to want to help Mrs. Jenkins. I'm sure she'll appreciate it once we find her. We may also need to help her clean the inside of the place. Whoever broke in did a lot of damage."

"You don't say." Bill frowned. "I'd hate for her to come back and have to deal with that. That would be awful."

Sarah nodded. "Well, we should be on our way. Enjoy your day, Bill. Thank you for Whiskey's treat."

A few minutes later they entered Java and Juice and at the tinkle of the bell on the door, all eyes turned toward Sarah and Whiskey. "Good morning, everyone," Sarah called out. Ginger was nowhere to be seen so Sarah figured she was busy in the kitchen.

A few people wished her good morning in return. Walter and Wendy Parks sat against the far wall eating breakfast. Walter waved her over while Whiskey, with his tail held high, beelined for the counter and Jared.

Sarah heard Jared say, "Great catch," as she got to the Parks' table. Walter motioned for her to bend down to their level and when she did, they leaned toward her and their voices were barely above a whisper.

"Got called out at two this morning, accident on the interstate. Two kids going too fast and hit a tree. I think they were joyriding." Walter paused.

"In a stolen car," Wendy said.

Walter nodded his head once. "A Buick." He stared into Sarah's eyes, like he was trying to transmit the information via telepathy.

"A blue one," Wendy added.

"Oh," Sarah said. "I didn't realize it was missing."

"Neither did the police. But you didn't hear that from us."

Mrs. Jenkins' garage was detached from her house and had no windows, so it was impossible to tell from the outside what was or was not inside it.

"Did you notice any cans of spray paint in the vehicle?"

"No," Wendy said.

"And the teens, are they okay?"

Walter's eyes darkened and his mouth was downturned. "The one may not make it. The other is critical but stable. They are local, but word hasn't gotten around yet."

Wendy's eyes filled with tears. "All the years we've been doing this, and it still affects me."

Sarah put a hand over Wendy's. "You have a good heart. You both do. Thank you for the information." She walked toward the counter and wondered what to make of this latest piece of the puzzle. *Did the kids know Mrs. Jenkins was missing so they took her car as a crime of opportunity? Or did they find it somewhere other than Mrs.*

Jenkins' garage and hotwire it?

"What'll it be today, mi'lady?" Jared asked, as if he could sense she could use her mood lightened. He grinned at her.

Sarah returned his smile. "Good morning, Jared." She handed him her empty to-go mug for the coffee and then ordered a ham and cheese croissant for breakfast and two Thai chicken and papaya salads for lunch. As she handed him her credit card, an idea came to her. "Hey Jared, are you busy around six today?"

His eyes widened so she quickly added, "I'm up for a little adventure and thought you might want to join."

"I always say yes to adventure. Or I mostly say yes." He chuckled.

"Great." Sarah looked around the café and decided she didn't want anyone to overhear her. She added, "I'll text you the details. Thanks. And see you later."

Sarah and Whiskey walked the last few blocks to the Coiffure to find that Emily was already there, the front door was unlocked, and Kai was watching his recently adopted Shibu Inu's nails get trimmed. Momo, as Kai explained he named her, rested on her belly with her paws outstretched like she was admiring her manicure.

Whiskey rubbed against Kai's leg and he murmured something to the dog in Japanese. Whiskey must have approved as he sat on Kai's foot, facing Momo, and waited.

"Hey, you're just the person I wanted to see," Sarah said, relishing her good fortune. Now she wouldn't have to try to hunt him down between classes at the dojo. "I don't know if you know, but I live next door to Janice Jenkins."

Kai said he did know that, as it was a small town. And then he laughed showing beautiful teeth.

The question of who his dentist was buzzed through Sarah's mind as fast and fleeting as a hummingbird, but she told herself to focus. "I was told by two different people that she wanted to take a self-defense class with you. Did she do that?"

Kai ran one hand through his straight black hair. "She signed up, but the course started two days ago, so...well, you know that she wasn't able to attend."

Sarah thought, *that is putting it delicately.*

"Did she tell you why she wanted to study self-defense?"

"Just that she wanted to update her skills." He shrugged. "She said almost fifty years ago she reached black belt level in judo, but she hadn't practiced in too long. She said she's done some online tai chi videos, but that isn't the same. Judo's purpose is to strengthen the body by practicing attack and defense. Tai chi is to improve energy levels and to increase flexibility and strength. They are very different."

"Yes," Sarah said. "I understand." And she wondered if the years ago judo had helped Mrs. Jenkins in whatever happened to her. "Did she happen to mention where she studied judo?"

Kai shook his head. "No, and I didn't ask." He looked at his dog for a beat and then back at Sarah. "But I have wondered if she had had a refresher...well...if things might have turned out differently." He frowned down at his shoes and Whiskey who was still sitting on one of his feet.

"I have wondered that, too," Sarah admitted.

Emily finished with Momo and said, "Who's a good girl?" And

gave the dog a freeze-dried liver treat.

When Whiskey saw that, he picked his butt up off of Kai and walked under the counter to beg for a treat from Emily, who laughed at him, before handing one over. He snatched it like a piranha with a minnow, one bite and it was gone.

Kai said, "I hope the police find her soon. The whole thing is terrible." Then he handed a ten and a five to Emily and told her he needed no change.

"Thank you," Emily said. "You're very generous."

With Momo now safely on the ground and her leash in his hand, Kai bid them both, "Good day," and bowed slightly, which Sarah returned.

Sarah opened the counter and walked through and then stashed the salads in the fridge. "You're an early bird today," she said.

"I couldn't sleep. I spent part of the night using that AI program on the photo of the woman on the ship. I think that ship's name was Victoria or maybe it was Astoria, something that ended in a -toria. If you zoom in on the photo you can barely make that out. And believe me, I've spent way too much time with that photo." She pushed a black and pink curl from her eyes.

"Are those actual ship names?" Sarah opened her laptop like she was going to look it up, but Emily stopped her with a "Yes. I did the research."

Sarah bent over the computer again and started to type "ship manifests" and then paused. Emily had been looking over her shoulder. She said, "I already did that too. The Astoria would have been in the 1940s. If Mrs. Jenkins is close to eighty, that may have been too early.

Ships named Victoria were many. One of the most famous ones was a ferry that sunk in 1953." Emily paused.

The door to the Coiffure opened and a lhaso apso named Lola trotted into the waiting area pulling her human companion behind her. Sylvia, wearing jeans and an oversized grey crewneck sweater, was in her sixties but frail from fighting cancer.

Emily scooped Lola up in her arms, so the dog didn't pull Sylvia over. "She's a rambunctious girl. And how are you today, Ms. Kyle?"

"Feel better than I have in months," Sylvia said.

Sarah noticed she had more color in her cheeks, and that it wasn't rouge. "You do look good," she said.

"Thank you. I finished treatment last month and there's no sign of the cancer. That's giving me hope."

"That's such wonderful news!" Sarah went into the waiting area to give Sylvia a hug, and Emily followed and gave Ms. Kyle a side-hug because she still had a squirming dog in her arms. "Give us a couple of hours with Lola," she said.

"Of course. I have some errands to run anyway. Thank you."

After Sylvia had left, Sarah said, "I'm so happy for her. And we could also use some good news right now." Then she filled Emily in on everything that had happened this morning since Robert's five a.m. wake up call, while Emily washed Lola and Whiskey supervised. When Sarah finished, she asked, "Did the AI match the woman on the ship to anyone?"

"It gave a number of possibilities but not exact matches and none of them were named Janice Jenkins or look like the current person we know by that name."

"Frustrating," Sarah said. "Though I wonder if the photo was meant to send people on a wild goose chase."

"Who knows," Emily said, rinsing Lola, whose long golden coat hung in wet clumps around her body. She looked like she shrunk three sizes in the wash. Emily toweled her off and put her on the grooming table before running a wide tooth comb down the dog to part her hair in the middle from the crown of her head to her backside.

Pat, from Cottageville Animal Rescue, walked through the door wearing a CAR branded polo shirt, and carrying a lop rabbit in her arms. The rabbit's nose wiggled frenetically at the scent of the dogs. Whiskey went into the waiting room to have a closer look and the rabbit tried to climb atop Pat's shoulder to safety.

"Whiskey, come here. You're scaring the rabbit. It doesn't know you are friendly."

Whiskey flattened his ears and returned to Sarah's side.

"Cute bunny," Emily said, over the hum of the blow dryer.

"Thanks. We just got it in, but its nails need a trim. Can you do it, Sarah?"

"Of course. Just put it on the counter. Does it have a name yet?"

"One of my kids named it Lopsy and would like us to keep it. But you know how it is. We can't keep them all."

"That's for sure," Sarah said as she clipped the docile rabbit's nails one by one.

When she got done, Pat asked, "What do I owe you?"

Sarah waved her hand and said, "Gratis. You're doing good work. Thank you for thinking of us. And I'll ask around if anyone wants a rabbit. It sure is cute."

CHAPTER FOURTEEN

At six o'clock, after stopping home, inhaling a microwave burrito, feeding Whiskey, and changing into a sweatshirt and hiking boots, Sarah and Whiskey met Jared on the street in front of Mrs. Jenkins' house. Sarah had packed some fruit and protein bars and two bottles of water for the humans and a refillable dog water bottle with flip down trough for Whiskey. Those and a couple of flashlights with fresh batteries, plus a cannister of pepper spray, were in her backpack.

"It occurred to me that the graffiti creators could have come down the street but may have fled through the woods. And if that is the case, I thought since we had recently been in the woods, that maybe we'd be able to tell if anything had changed."

"Good thinking," Jared said. "And I'm glad you didn't decide to investigate this on your own." He smiled at her, so Sarah took his comment as care and not a reprimand.

"I figure we have a couple of hours before it gets dark." She dug the flashlights out of the backpack anyway and handed one to him. The hefty metal flashlight could double as a weapon, if need be, but then again, Whiskey might be the best deterrent or weapon of all, Sarah mused to herself.

As they walked around Mrs. Jenkins' house, Sarah searched for grass that had been trampled or droplets of paint—anything to provide them with some direction. "Do you smell anyone, boy? Sarah asked Whiskey. He was following his nose as usual, but Sarah had no idea if he was on the trail of a squirrel, a raccoon, or a person. He zigged one way in the backyard and then another. He even went in a circle before they made it to the woods at the back of the property.

Whiskey wove through the trees with Sarah and Jared walking single file but close together. "I think this is the same path we went on the last time," Jared said, pointing to the broken tree branches.

"Looks like it," Sarah said. Her eyes scanned the dried leaves and small sticks that crunched under her feet. She eyed every plant they passed, searching for anything amiss.

"What did you study at university?" Jared asked.

"Business and communications. Double major."

"What made you open the Coiffure?"

"I've always loved animals," Sarah said, while stepping over a downed tree trunk. "When my grandmother got sick and I came to stay with her, I realized Cottageville didn't have a groomer. I worked at one in Seattle to pay my way through school. It was work I enjoyed and I was good at. So, I figured, why not stay here and open one. I mean after I found out she had left me the house. I always liked coming here as a kid, and everyone has been so nice to me, accepted me as a local." Sarah looked back over her shoulder at him and smiled. "What about you?"

"Me? Why I've always wanted to be a knight in shining armor, in service to mi'lady," Jared joked.

Whiskey picked up the pace as he tracked a scent, so Sarah and Jared walked faster.

"Sure you have," Sarah said, "just as working at Java and Juice is your dream come true."

"Touché. Actually, I came across this place on a road trip after college. It's a great location to access nature and hiking trails, and the cost of living is just right for me. You know I work with Ginger because I'm saving for a house, right? But I'm actually an illustrator and writer."

"I heard a rumor about that, but no one seemed to know what you wrote."

"So, you've asked around, have you?" Jared teased.

"Only when it's come up," Sarah admitted, feeling her face flush.

"I write and draw comic books, mostly, and I've done two graphic novels that are making the rounds of publishers."

"That's so cool."

"The comic books are. I enjoy them. My stuff isn't huge here, but I have a following in Germany and a bit of Asia."

Sarah did a one-eighty quickly. "Seriously?" she asked as Jared almost ran into her. He reached his hands out on either side of her biceps so that they both didn't fall over.

"Yes, seriously. When I'm away from the café occasionally, it's usually because I'm at ComicCon or something like that."

"I had no idea," Sarah said, wondering why Ginger never mentioned it. Or had she? Sarah racked her brain trying to remember.

"Yes, I'm that big of a dweeb," Jared joked.

"I don't think that's dweeby at all. You're very creative and doing what you want. I think that's great, and that it is this town that lets us or helps us thrive. What did you study in college?"

"Art, well drawing, and English. I think we moved to Cottageville around the same time, you know. Like a little over six years ago."

"Oh nice," Sarah said. "Whiskey, what are you doing?" Sarah's attention shifted to her dog. He had stopped and started digging through the leaves and into the dirt. Soil and bits of forest floor flew towards Sarah's legs with every frantic scratch of his paws.

Suddenly he stopped and plunged his head into the hole he had dug. He jerked his head back and Sarah saw bones and a bit of decay. "Drop it," she commanded.

Whiskey turned his head away from her with the dead thing still clamped in his jaws. Sarah tried to reach for it, but Whiskey darted away from her.

Jared laughed. "I think he's saying, 'It's mine. Get your own.'"

"Most likely," Sarah said. "I hope it doesn't make him sick."

"Yeah, that wouldn't be good."

Whiskey ran ahead to what looked like a clearing through the trees. When Sarah and Jared exited the woods, they stepped into a field of tall grass with some kind of rounded tower in the center. "Is that a water tower?" Sarah asked.

"Not sure." Jared walked side by side with her now. And as they got closer to the tower, they noticed black spray paint on the base of the white tower. They weren't large, but the letters JUNE in shaky block capitals glared back at them.

"It's May," Sarah said as Whiskey sniffed and circled the base of the tower; his dug-up prize was now nowhere in sight, so Sarah figured it was in his stomach. She hoped it didn't give him bad gas. Sometimes dog farts were the worst.

"It's a strange thing to write," Jared said. He pulled out his phone and used the GPS to capture the coordinates of where they were. "The paint color and sheen are the same as at Mrs. Jenkins' though."

"It is. Are you sending a text to the chief?"

"Not yet. I'd like to drink some of the water you brought for me, and then let's walk a few paces that way." He pointed past the tower to another part of the field.

Sarah gave him a bottle of water and she opened one for herself. She also flipped the trough on Whiskey's bottle and squeezed water into it. He lapped the water like he was racing Jared to see who could finish first...though Jared wasn't racing or chugging. He took a few sips and then slipped the bottle into the back pocket of his jeans.

When they walked twenty feet past the water tower, a bit of shine caught Jared's eye. He bent down and then stood upright with two empty cans of black enamel spray paint.

"Prints," Sarah reminded.

"Oh yeah," Jared said, dropping the cans. "And now it is time to text the chief."

Since Sarah had been in continual contact with Chief Order, she sent him the text. The text read, "I am at the water tower and found black enamel spray cans and writing. The word June has been sprayed on the tower."

Within seconds the chief called Sarah. "Sarah, I really appreciate all the effort you are putting into the search, but you need to be careful. This whole ordeal is getting out of hand and there are too many unknowns for you to be out by yourself this close to dark."

"Thank you for your concern, chief," Sarah responded, a little irritated but thankful that the chief genuinely cared. "I am actually here with Whiskey and Jared, so I am in good hands, or should I say paws. I'll text you the GPS coordinates. It would be good if you came out here and took a look around."

"Okay," replied the chief, "I will be there as soon as I can. In the meantime, please stay put and don't go anywhere until I get there."

"Deal. See you soon." *Did the chief know who he was talking to,* Sarah wondered. *There's no way we are going to stand here and do nothing!* Sarah began walking around the water tower, and Jared and Whiskey followed her like they were a merry band of investigators. "There has to be more clues here, Jared."

Before Jared could respond, Sarah expressed her thoughts aloud. "Why would someone come out here and spray paint June on the tower? Why here of all places? What's going on? Where is Mrs. Jenkins?"

The three of them walked around the tower, but now Whisky

was leading the way. Jared and Sarah, both with minds racing like greyhounds after rabbits, were silent as they walked with eyes glued to the ground, believing they would stumble across something that could lead them to Mrs. Jenkins.

Before long Chief Order came through the trees and toward the tower, accompanied by Officer John Beams. Whiskey gave a friendly woof and darted off to greet them. "Hello, Whiskey," both the chief and Officer Beams said simultaneously.

"Find anything else?" the chief asked. His hair was ruffled and his skin was pale. Sarah felt sorry for him. He looked like he had had a rough day.

"Nothing yet," replied Jared. "But we know there has to be more here than just the word June and the two spray cans."

Beams also looked more tired than a sheepdog during shearing season. He took some photos of the cans and then picked them up using the evidence bags and zipped the bags closed, while the chief stared at the spray painting on the tower. "It isn't artistic enough for tagging," the chief said.

"Not at all," Jared agreed.

Sarah wondered if he had done any of that in his youth since tagging looked like some comic book artwork but thought it best not to ask him in front of the chief.

Beams suggested they spread out and walk in wide circles from the tower outward. So they each picked a direction and searched the ground. Whiskey tagged along with Sarah, keeping close at her heel. They stumbled across the usual gum wrappers, a hair tie, and a mud-encrusted empty plastic bottle but found nothing that screamed "clue".

Daylight was fading fast, so the chief shouted that they should walk for another five minutes and then head back.

Sarah didn't want to stop. She'd been on an adrenaline high, like when a dog chases a cat, since they saw the tower and spotted the cans, but she knew it was best to listen to the chief. Plus, if she was honest with herself, she was starting to tire. The last few days had been long and emotionally draining.

As each of them finished searching, they gravitated to the place on the tower that screamed "June", as if they were magnets being pulled by an opposing force. No one had said, "Hey, let's meet over at the word June," but they all walked to that point and stopped.

As if they were speaking to him, Jared stared at the letters spray painted in black on the white tower. The chief and Beams, with their backs to the tower, searched the trees and field and far off places, like they were scoping the area to see if they were being watched. Sarah sat down with her back against one of tower supports, with her feet flat on the ground, and her knees pulled up to her chest. She shut her eyes, placed her forehead on her knees and wrapped her arms around her legs. She wondered if the ground would speak to her, or if she could feel the energy of the people who had passed here before. Whiskey, not wanting to be left out, put his cold, wet nose under Sarah's arm next to her left knee. Sarah didn't lift her head or acknowledge Whiskey's presence, but she felt grounded by him. She was certain there was more, that they were missing something. But she couldn't quite grasp what it was.

Chief Order turned to Sarah to suggest that they be on their way. As he looked down at her, he noticed what looked like a piece of paper close to where Sarah was sitting up against the tower. "Sarah, what is that paper next to you?"

Lifting her head from her arms and knees, Sarah looked up at the chief and followed his eyes to where they were fixed. She leaned over to her right, away from where Whiskey still sat close to her, reached out her hand, and picked up the paper.

But it wasn't paper. It was an old, worn, ripped photograph. The tear cut from the upper right corner diagonally to the left middle section of the photo. The photo appeared to contain two women, but because of the tear, only the bottom two-thirds of them were in the photograph. In the twilight, it was difficult to make out any details.

"I wonder who is in this picture and how it got here," Sarah said, handing the photo to Officer Beams, who put it into an evidence bag.

"I am not sure, but we need to get out of here. It's too dark and it could get dangerous," said the chief.

Jared, no longer staring at the word on the tower but at Sarah, responded to the chief's suggestion. "Yes, we do need to get moving. We can look at the picture in more detail later."

With that, Jared reached out his hand to help Sarah to her feet and said, "Mi'lady."

Sarah chuckled and said, "Thank you, my lord."

Whiskey led the way back toward the trees. Sarah kept track of him by illuminating the tip of his tail with her flashlight. They made their way slowly, careful where they stepped, but eventually they came to the clearing that was Mrs. Jenkins' backyard and said their goodnights.

CHAPTER FIFTEEN

Exhausted and not having consumed enough coffee yet, Sarah unlocked and pushed open the green front door of Carter's Canine Coiffure and made her way to the counter, while Whiskey made his way to the back room. Grabbing the schedule, she noted the day was full of appointments with some of her most challenging furry clients. *This is going to be an exceptionally long day,* Sarah thought. As she was setting the appointment book on the counter, in walked Emily, who seemed more excited than usual. "Hey Em, how are you today?"

"Great," responded Emily. "Since 5 p.m. last night, my phone hasn't stopped dinging. Not one T but two have been texting me."

Sara laughed. "How does it feel to have two guys interested in you?"

Emily rolled her eyes, smiled, and said, "It's kind of funny. Taylor and Travis are nothing alike, but I find them both attractive and easy to talk to. Even Taylor's poor use of English strikes me as cute, as much as I want to correct him. But Travis is gorgeous and smart, and I want to run my fingers through his wavy hair. You wouldn't think he's my type, but there's something about him that rocks."

"Well," Sarah started to respond, "I ..." Her sentence was cut short as the chief walked in. "Good morning, Chief, you get any rest last night?"

"Not much, not much at all. I wanted to ask for your help before the day got too busy. I know you mentioned something about using AI in your search for Mrs. Jenkins, so I was wondering if I could leave some pictures with you and Emily. The receptionist at the station took individual pictures of each piece of jewelry we've found in this case, and I have the two photographs. Can I leave them with you and see what your AI magic discovers?"

"Sure, Chief. We have a busy day, but we will get on it right away," responded Sarah.

The chief reached into his inner coat pocket and pulled out a Ziplock gallon-size bag and handed it to Sarah. "Here you go, detective Sarah, let me know what you find." At that, the three laughed and the chief left.

Detective Sarah, Sarah thought, *I like that. I will be the next Nancy Drew.*

While Sarah prepped the work areas, Emily pulled her laptop

out of her bag and set it up. Sarah tried to focus on the appointments for the day and what she'd need handy, but her mind was more enthralled with the idea of detective work.

Whiskey let out a woof and headed toward the front door. Spike, a seventy-five-pound pit bull, and Tony, his 35-year-old never-married human, entered the waiting area. Tony was built like Spike. He didn't have a neck, but humungous traps, and his chest resembled a large, wooden bourbon barrel, like the ones used to age wine.

"Good morning, boys," said Sarah, as she made her way past the counter to greet them. Whiskey and Spike played, grabbing at each other's necks and ears. Spike didn't come in often, but Whiskey loved to rough house with him when he saw the dog. It was like one of those friendships where you don't see the other person very often, but when you do, you love your time together.

Emily came from behind the counter, greeted Spike and Tony, and took the leash from Tony's hand. "Come on, Spike, it's time to make you even more handsome than you are," said Emily.

As Emily walked to the back with Spike, Tony and Sarah small talked about Tony's gym, Big T's Fitness Center, and the new equipment they installed, but there was not any talk about Mrs. Jenkins. If Tony wasn't going to mention anything, Sarah didn't want to either. As they were saying their good-byes, Cory, a dainty yorkie came in for her bi-monthly treatment.

Before long, Emily and Sarah had washed and nail clipped five dogs and one extremely pregnant rabbit. And of course, Whiskey did his fair share of work as well. As the morning rush reached its peak, Sarah texted Ginger and ordered two salads with strawberry vinaigrette dressing and grilled salmon.

Within minutes, Jared arrived with the requested salads and two complimentary small smoothies. Jared flashed a friendly smile and said, "Mi'lady," as he handed Sarah the bag and set the smoothies on the counter.

"Thank you, my lord." Sarah smiled at Jared. She was aware that something in her was shifting regarding him. He no longer seemed like her brother.

Jared gave Sarah a huge grin and promised to meet her at her house tonight if she wanted to search again for clues or for Mrs. Jenkins. And then he bid them both, *"Adieu."*

Emily seized the between-client moment to eat her salad. She took pictures using her phone of the pictures that the chief brought, so she could airdrop them to her laptop. With the pictures now on her computer, Emily searched the internet using AI, trying to find out something, anything about the jewelry and who the people were in the photographs.

Sarah grabbed her food and smoothie and sat next to Emily. "Find anything yet?"

"This is going to be hard. We only have half of a picture with two people in it, and it's only from their chests down. And we have an old, dirty picture that's challenging to decipher."

"Well, we have twenty-five minutes before our next client arrives, let's eat and keep searching." The two sat in silence, which was broken only by a few slurps of their smoothies and crunches from the nuts on the salads. They studied image after image as they scrolled through the internet's endless amount of information.

Sarah had an idea; she went to the desk in the back office and searched through cabinets and drawers. The ruckus got Whiskey's attention, so he made his way to Sarah's side and gave a smaller, quiet bark, like he wanted to know: "Hey, what's up?"

Sarah looked down at him. "Whiskey, where is the magnifying glass? I know we have one somewhere."

As if he understood, Whiskey threw his snout in the air, barked—this time loudly,—and went straight to the end cabinet. He stood on his hind legs, placing his front paws on top of the cabinet and tried to open the middle drawer with his teeth.

Sarah said to herself, "You've got to be kidding me." She walked over to the cabinet and pulled out the drawer Whiskey was so intently trying to open. There, beneath some old folders and miscellaneous junk, was the magnifying glass.

Sarah scratched Whiskey's head and behind his ears, and said in a sweet, high-pitched voice, "You're such a good boy, yeah, such a good boy."

They returned to where Emily sat and searched on the computer. Reaching into the Ziplock bag, Sarah pulled out the pictures and began to look at them under the magnifying glass. She started with the rings, the ones she found at the house with the chief. One by one she studied them, looking for engravings, dates, anything that would give them more leads. After going over the jewelry photos, she began looking at the partial photograph she found last night and the one posted online. *There must be clues here,* Sarah thought. *Who are the people in these pictures?*

She combed millimeter by millimeter over the latest picture

they found, like she was using a metal detector to find something lost in the sand. Over and over it she moved the magnifying glass. *Come on, come on. There must be something here.*

"Ugh!" Sarah exclaimed.

"What's wrong?" Emily asked.

"Nothing, I just really thought we were going to find clues in these pictures. I sensed it. You know, like when you feel something is on the verge of happening or when your intuition kicks in?"

"That's interesting, because I felt it too. I believe we will find something, And Sarah, you never told me about last night. Where did you go? Was Jared with you? And where in the world did the new picture come from?"

Sarah's head was still bowed, one eye closed, and the other was open and peering through the lens of the magnifying glass. She wanted to go into the details of last night's adventure, but she was too exhausted and too intent on this photograph. Plus, their next client was due to arrive at any minute, so she wanted to deflect the question to a later time. Without ever lifting her head up from the lens and photograph, Sarah started, "Jared and I—there it is!"

"There what is?" Emily's voice exuded the excitement of a Siberian husky seeing a cat.

"There's the clue! I found it!" Whiskey barked once in agreement with Sarah's shout. With her eyes even more narrowly focused on the photograph, she put the hand not holding the magnifying glass out to Emily. "Emily, hand me the picture of the shiny gold ring with the big ruby."

Emily slid it over to her, so it was next to the photograph Sarah was staring at. Emily stood, hovering over Sarah, trying to see what she saw. She shifted back and forth, first looking over Sarah's right shoulder, then her left, but she couldn't see past Sarah's head to see what was so intriguing. With her voice pitched high like a Pomeranian's, Emily said, "The suspense is killing me. What do you see?"

Sarah joked, "When threatened by a vicious woman, remain calm and speak in cold, level tones!"

"Huh?" responded Emily.

Sarah realized immediately that Emily wasn't familiar with Nancy Drew. "Never mind but take a look at this." She handed Emily the magnifying glass and slid both pictures over to her. Sarah suggested that Emily study the gold ring with the ruby first before moving onto the picture that was torn in half.

Emily, now with one eye focused on the oversized lens, studied the beautiful ring. She could never see herself wearing a gold ring, especially not one with such a large, vibrant red stone. Emily was fond of silver jewelry and would much rather have a ring with a skull than a ring with a stone.

"You done yet? You get a good picture in your mind of the ring's details?" asked Sarah.

"Absolutely."

"Good, now look at the lady standing on the left. As you look at the picture, notice her right hand." Glee oozed from Sarah's voice.

"Holy crap! Sarah, it's the ring. It's the gold ring with the giant ruby that you found at Mrs. Jenkin's. "

Whiskey joined in the excitement, giving a few short, high-pitched barks.

Sarah thought, *He should be excited. If it weren't for him, no one would have known that something happened at Mrs. Jenrkin's house.*

Plus, Whiskey found the jewelry under the bed, which led Sarah to look under the mattress.

The front door opened, and George entered with a wet, filthy Chutney under his right arm. Recognizing that his human was too caught up in the pictures and didn't realize she had clients, Whiskey gave a woof, which caused Emily and Sarah to look up toward the waiting area.

"Hello, George." Sarah said. "Did I make a mistake and not put Chutney on the schedule for today?"

"Sarah, I'm sorry. We don't have an appointment, but I didn't know what else to do. Look at my poor little Chut. I let her out on the front porch and went back into the house to make myself a sandwich before I headed back to the grocery store. When I returned to let her in, she was rolling around in the mulch bed. The neighbor boy planted two dwarf cypress trees for us and placed new mulch around them. I think there might have been manure mixed in, because Chutney loved it and wouldn't stop rolling in it. I have to get back to the store, but I couldn't let Chutney in the house like this. Is there any way you could squeeze her in today?"

"Of course, we can, George." Sarah grabbed a towel off the shelf and walked over to George, placing the towel around Chutney's stinky and dirty little Chihuahua frame. She gently removed the dog from under George's arm and said, "Come with me, poop breath." To George she said, "We will see you before six, George. Have a good afternoon."

"Emily, "said Sarah, "hurry up and put the pictures and laptop away before the afternoon rush arrives. I will work on our favorite little Tasmanian devil. And please use my phone to text the chief and tell him what we found. Maybe he could swing by later if he's not busy."

Sarah placed Chutney in the tub and slid on the long, leather gloves she had purchased at Buck and Son Hardware. But for the bath, she put oversized rubber gloves over them so the water wouldn't destroy the leather. She was grateful that she had them. Sarah ran the water, adjusting the warm and cold faucets, being sure that the water was the appropriate temperature, while Emily finished putting the investigative tools away and texted the chief.

Whiskey could sense Chutney's panic, so he stood next to Sarah, on his hind legs, with his front paws up on the side of the tub. He did his best to calm down his little, filthy friend.

CHAPTER SIXTEEN

It was a long day, but it went by quickly. Sarah cleaned the front of the shop, while Emily mopped the floors and rinsed out the tubs. George arrived exactly at 5:59 p.m. to retrieve Chutney, who was content sleeping against Whiskey on the floor by the front counter.

"You are a life savior, Sarah. How much do I owe you?" asked George.

"Forty."

George reached into his pocket and pulled out a crisp fifty-dollar bill and handed it to Sarah.

"Thank you. I really appreciate you getting me out of this bind. Keep the change and here, I brought you a bag of fresh produce. I know you love organic veggies, so here are carrots, bell peppers, and a butternut squash."

"Thank you, George. That's very kind of you."

George picked Chutney up off the floor, thanked Sarah again, and left.

Sarah thought, *It's after six and I still haven't heard anything from the chief. He must have had a busy day as well.* No sooner than that thought left her mind, her cell phone began to vibrate. Reaching into the front pocket of her apron, Sarah pulled out her phone and saw it was the chief. "Hello, Chief. How are you?"

"I'm fine, but my mouth is numb. I've been sitting in an uncomfortable dentist chair all afternoon, fixing a crown that recently cracked. That's why I haven't been able to stop by. I'm just leaving the dentist now."

"I'm sorry Chief, the dentist is my least favorite place in the world."

The chief, slurring a little from the Novocain, asked if he should stop at the Coiffure or wait until the morning.

Sarah, anxious to share the new details, encouraged the chief to come by. As Sarah disconnected the call with the chief, Jared walked in.

"I saw you were still here, so I came here instead of your house," said Jared. He had changed into ripped jeans, an evergreen-colored t-shirt, and a gray sweatshirt was tied around his waist.

In her excitement about the clue, Sarah grabbed Jared's right forearm. "I'm glad you are here. I can't wait to tell you what we found."

Emily, picking up her backpack and the remainder of her salad, said, "I'd love to hang with you, but my homework is calling."

Jokingly, Sarah asked, "Are you sure it's not one of the T's calling?"

"Very funny. I'll see you in the morning. Goodnight, Whiskey," Emily said, as she exited the front door.

Turning her attention back to Jared and talking as fast as a middle schooler giving a speech, Sarah went through the details of their discovery.

"Can you believe it, Jared? The ring I found at Mrs. Jenkin's house is the same ring that someone is wearing in the photograph we found last night. There is no way that's a coincidence."

With his fingers intertwined and his hands resting on the top of his head, Jared said, "That's wild, Sarah. This is the most excitement this town has had in years, and we are in the epicenter of it. This is either going to end awesome or, well, ummm, not so good." Jared frowned and his demeanor changed drastically with that last comment.

"What's that supposed to mean?" Sarah felt every muscle in her body tense.

Whiskey must have sensed the shift because he stood between them and looked from Sarah to Jared and back again.

Jared simmered over his thoughts before responding. "It would be one thing if Mrs. Jenkin's house was broken into, but it was broken into, ransacked, and she's missing. She's missing, and people just don't go missing from Cottageville. And not only is she missing, but no one knows anything about her, the woman hasn't left a footprint anywhere. Then you find expensive jewelry in her house, wait, not just expensive jewelry, because a lot of people have expensive jewelry, but what is probably antique jewelry and a lot of it. Oh yeah, did I mention that her car was stolen, someone spray painted messages on her house, an anonymous person posted a picture online and says nasty things about Mrs. Jenkins, and now, last night, we find the word JUNE painted on the water tower and discover part of picture next to the tower. Everything seems off, Sarah. Do you think it was by chance we found that photograph last night? I mean really think about it. I bet someone wanted us to find it. This is no longer a children's mystery novel. I feel like we are living a Scooby-Doo episode, and I'm Shaggy, you are Daphne, and of course Whiskey is Scooby!"

Sarah snort-laughed. And that made Jared crack up until the two of them were laughing. Whiskey joined with short, high-pitched barks, and he turned in circles around them.

"What am I missing? I could sure use a good laugh," said the chief as he entered the shop.

"It wouldn't be funny if we told you, Chief. It was an in-the-moment thing," Jared said.

The three of them gravitated to the front counter, each finding their own way to lean into it for support.

Sarah, without an intro or prelude, went straight to the climax of events. "The gold ring with the giant red ruby we found at Mrs. Jenkin's house is the same ring one of the women is wearing in the picture we found last night."

The chief's face turned pale, and he leaned over the counter to hold himself up.

"Chief, are you alright?" Concern seeped from Jared, and he

put a hand toward the chief, like he would catch him if he fainted.

"I'm not sure. I think it's the combination of Novocain, painkillers, and what you just said. I feel dizzy and nauseous."

"Sarah," said Jared, "lock up the shop and head home. I will drive the chief home in his cruiser, then head over to your place."

Sarah went to the door and held it open as Jared put the chief's left arm over his right shoulder and helped him through the door, like a football player helping an injured teammate off the field. They hobbled across the street where Jared assisted the chief in getting into the passenger side of his cruiser. Whiskey sat on the sidewalk, supervising like a foreman on a construction site. As Jared and the chief rolled away, Sarah stepped back into the shop, turned off the lights, and locked the front door.

"Home we go, Whiskey," said Sarah.

Whiskey and Sarah walked through town toward home, greeting other shop owners that were closing for the day, and Whiskey, of course, lifted his leg on numerous occasions to mark his territory.

As they were passing Robert Wise's house, Sarah noticed a man with a large gorgeous German shepherd walking past Mrs. Jenkin's house and towards them on the sidewalk. Whiskey noticed them too and started with a deep, soft growl. "Whiskey, stop that," demanded Sarah.

As they strolled toward each other, Sarah slid to the right of the sidewalk. *Who is this guy? I've never seen this dog before. I would surely recognize him if I had,* Sarah thought.

In accented English, Sarah heard, "Lovely cattle dog!"

"Thank you," Sarah responded, "Very handsome shepherd."

"*Danke*," said the man.

Whiskey and the shepherd both posted themselves in between their humans. It was odd behavior for Whiskey, Sarah thought. He was usually outgoing and loving, but he did not move from this spot or take his eyes off the man standing in front of him.

"What is his name?" asked the man.

"Whiskey," said Sarah. Whiskey gave a quick woof when he heard his name.

"What's your dog's name?" asked Sarah.

"Arminius, named after a famous chieftain in my motherland," responded the man.

Wanting to end this awkward encounter, Sarah said, "Cool name. It was nice talking, but we need to be on our way."

"Oh, okay," responded the man. "What is your name?"

Do I really want to tell him my name? This is a small town, and we know everyone but him. But Sarah's manners from her upbringing overrode her caution.

Extending her right hand, Sarah said, "My name is Sarah, and I own Carter's Canine Coiffure. If you ever want to bring Arminius by, we will take great care of him."

"Thank you, Sarah. My name is Fritz."

"Nice to meet you, Fritz."

Sarah encouraged Whiskey to walk again but they were interrupted by Fritz.

"Before you go, do you know who owns this house?"

"Why do you ask?" Suspicion raised the hairs of Sarah's arms.

Fritz began, "Arminius and I are moving to Cottageville and

are looking to buy a house. I walked past this one, and since there's spray painted words on it, I figured it was abandoned. So, we walked around it and noticed there were problems around the back, with the screen door and door. I've purchased houses in many small towns, and this looks a lot like the ones I like to buy."

A chill ran down Sarah's spine. "It's not for sale, the owner has been out of town."

"Oh, great. You know the owner. How can I contact her?"

Her? thought Sarah. *I never said, her. I said the owner is out of town.* She made mental notes of the man's clothes, his eye color, and his shoes. She had learned during a police visit to her university in Seattle that if she were ever a victim of a crime to pay attention to a person's shoes. Sweatshirts and masks were easy to change, but most robbers and pickpockets never considered changing their shoes after committing a crime.

"Hey guys," Jared said from twenty yards down the walk.

"Hey, Jared!" yelled Sarah.

"Jared, I want you to meet Fritz and Arminius, they are moving to Cottageville." Sarah spoke loud enough for her voice to carry.

"Great." Jared approached them on the sidewalk. "Cottageville is an amazing place." Jared sensed the tension and saw the dogs in a standoff. "Nice to meet you, Fritz, and nice to meet you too, Arminius. What a good-looking dog! I hate to meet and run, but Sarah, we are going to be late. We need to go."

"Yes, we don't want to be late. Nice to meet you, Fritz. Have a good night," Sarah said. "Let's go, Whiskey."

Whiskey let out a woof, threw his head back, communicating

to Arminius that this was his part of town, and followed after Jared and Sarah.

"Slow down, Sarah, and don't go to your house. Keep walking," Jared whispered.

The three of them walked five minutes past the house in silence, and then turned around and started walking back.

"Who was that guy?" asked Jared. "He was at least six-foot-three, and his silver beard and blondish silver hair gave him the appearance of a movie star. How old do you think he is?"

"Fifty-five or sixty. He may look like a movie star, but he gave me the creeps. I'll give you that he looks distinguished, but he gives off bad vibes."

"For sure," said Jared.

"He even told me that he was scoping out Mrs. Jenkins' house. And you know what? When he asked about the house, I told him the owner was out of town and he said, 'Oh, you know her?' Jared, I never told him the owner was a woman. There is something very off about that man and why he is here in our town."

Seeing that Fritz and Arminius were no longer in sight, they made a dash to the front door, entered the house, and made sure the front door was locked

"Jared, if Fritz knows Mrs. Jenkins in the owner of the house, that means he probably knows I live here, too. Maybe it wasn't a coincidence that our paths crossed, but maybe he was actually waiting for me."

Now very frightened, Sarah asked, "What would have happened if you didn't arrive when you did? What were Fritz's intentions tonight?

Jared, I'm scared."

"Don't be scared, Sarah, Whiskey is here with you and so am I."

Jared's words felt good, like a warm blanket on a brisk fall evening.

CHAPTER SEVENTEEN

Sarah was abruptly awakened by a knocking on the front door. It sounded urgent, like a child banging on the door when they must pee, but the bathroom is occupied. Whiskey beelined to the door and barked like an intruder was about.

"Whiskey, it's me, Emily. Whiskey, it's me."

Sarah made her way to the bathroom, slipped on her robe, and went towards the door.

"Who is it, Whiskey?" asked Sarah.

Sarah could hear Emily's voice now. "Whiskey. Sarah. It's Emily."

Unlocking the door, Sarah opened it and let Emily in.

"Sorry to get you up, but I woke up at four and couldn't go back to sleep. So, I decided to do more searching with AI and the web." As excited as a five-year-old at Christmas, Emily continued, "You aren't going to believe what I found. That's why I'm here. I couldn't wait to show you."

Taking off her backpack and pulling out her computer, Emily walked toward the couch and sat down. With her laptop on her legs and backpack on the floor next to her, Emily opened documents she had saved on her desktop.

"Emily, while you do that, I am going to let Whiskey out, get dressed, and make coffee," Sarah said.

Not sure if Emily even heard her, Sarah let Whiskey out, started the coffee maker in the kitchen, then went into her bathroom and shut the door. While Sarah was in the bathroom, Emily let Whiskey in, put breakfast in his bowl, and poured two cups of coffee, one in Emily's favorite coffee mug, which looked homemade and had a picture of Whiskey on it, and the other in Sarah's faithful tumbler. Emily grabbed her coffee and slowly made her way back to the sofa. She sipped her coffee and tapped her fingers while waiting for Sarah.

Walking into the living room, dressed in black yoga tights, an oversized ink blue sweatshirt with the words *Dog's Best Friend,* and with her hair still wet, Sarah said, "Okay, Em, show me what you got!"

"Sit down next to me and look at this," said Emily. "Here are the pictures of the jewelry we have." She reached up and put her left index finger on the screen. "Now look at these pictures, they are one in the same! Sarah, the jewelry that ended up in our little town was stolen from the Pforzheim Jewelry Musuem in June 1982. It's been missing for forty-one years!"

"No way! No stinking way!" exclaimed Sarah. "Can you find some articles about the robbery while I call the chief?"

"Already have them saved in my favorites," responded Emily.

Sarah paced back and forth with her phone to her ear. "Come on, Chief. Answer the phone."

"Good morning, Sarah."

Without any greeting, Sarah rushed into the latest findings and everything that had happened—including her run-in with the weird dude and the theft from a museum in Germany of all places, she ended with, "Chief, this is big. I think we might be trying to swim in quicksand, but we keep sinking deeper and deeper."

The chief let loose an audible sigh. "It's going to be okay. We'll figure this all out. I am going to head to the station and make some calls. You and Emily need to go about your day just like it is any other day. I will touch base with you in a few hours."

"I will try, Chief, but—" said Sarah.

"Talk soon," replied Chief Order and then he disconnected.

"What did the chief say?" asked Emily.

"Not much, just that we need to stick to our normal routine and get to work," said Sarah.

Emily slid the laptop back into her backpack and walked her coffee mug back to the kitchen, rinsed it, and set it on the countertop, while Sarah gathered her belongings and topped off her tumbler. As they stepped through the front door onto the porch, Sarah turned to lock the door and thought, *You can do this. You are adventurous, independent, and strong. You are going to solve this mystery.*

Besides the usual morning greetings to some of their favorite townspeople, not a word was spoken between Sarah and Emily. Mentally, they were painstakingly trying to fit the pieces together, like constructing a thousand-piece puzzle without seeing the box. Arriving at Java and Juice, but before going in, Sarah asked Emily what she wanted and asked her to go open the Coiffure and get prepped while she grabbed some breakfast and lunch for both of them.

Sarah pushed open the painted red door on Java and Juice, which tinkled the brass bell louder than usual. Ginger was busy attending to a customer; her blond curly hair was pulled back and through the hole above her Java and Juice logoed trucker's cap closure. Sarah admired how great Ginger looked in the hat.

A few of the regulars stood patiently in line, awaiting their turn to order fresh baked pastries and coffee.

Whiskey parked himself next to the counter and waited while Sarah eyed the delicious eclairs, croissants, muffins, and cake-style donuts. Emily wanted the chocolate croissant, which was Sarah's favorite, but Sarah wanted something different today. She walked to the end of the line and waited while Jared filled the orders of the customers in front of her and Whiskey, and then Jared greeted them with a warm smile.

"What's up, Whiskey!" he said, reaching his hand over the counter to rub the cattle dog's ears.

Jared then gave him one of Ginger's homemade chicken bone-shaped dog treats. Whiskey gave Jared a cattle dog smile, black gums gleaming.

"And what will you have today, mi' lady Drew?" Jared asked, then laughed.

"Mi' lady Drew, huh. Really more like Sherlock Holmes."

They both chuckled.

"The chocolate croissant for Emily, my lord, and a cinnamon crumb cake for me."

"No coffee today?" asked Jared.

"I topped it off before leaving the house. Emily showed up at the butt-crack of dawn to show me what she found, but I will tell you about it later. Too many ears in here."

"Gotcha," replied Jared.

Sarah handed Jared a $20 bill in exchange for a white paper bag with the Java and Juice logo stamped on it in black ink.

"I'll be right back with your change, "Jared said.

Sarah responded, "Don't be silly. Throw it in the tip jar and be sure to come by the Coiffure when you get a chance."

"Will do. See you later."

"Come on, Whiskey," Sarah said.

"Bye, Whiskey," Jared said.

Sarah turned around and headed toward the front door, smiling at the locals as she made her way out of the cafe with Whiskey right behind her. Sarah talked to Whiskey as they walked to their business. She bounced ideas and theories off him, as if he was her BFF. Because, well, he was, besides Ginger.

From a block away, Sarah saw the tall man and large German shepherd standing outside the Coiffure.

"Oh crap. It's Fritz. Whiskey, walk closer to me."

Sarah and Whiskey approached Fritz and Arminius and greeted them in a way that Sarah hoped hid how she really felt. "Good morning, Fritz. How are you and Arminius today?"

"Very well, Sarah. *Danke.* How are you and Whiskey?"

"Fine. What brings you to Carter's Canine Coiffure?"

Fritz, with his height and his broad shoulders, appeared to be towering over Sarah. He reminded her that she invited him to bring Arminius for grooming.

"Yes, yes, of course. We have a full morning, but if you leave Arminius with us, I will be sure we get to him by one." Sarah swallowed the acid her nerves had caused to reflux.

"Perfect," responded Fritz. "I am staying at the Whispering Pines Bed and Breakfast across town. However, I'm going to hang around town and shop for a time." Reaching into his front right pants pocket, Fritz pulled out his business card and handed it to Sarah. "My mobile number is on the card. Call me when Arminius is ready to be picked up."

"Okay." Sarah reached out for the card and for Arminius' leash. "I'll take Arminius, too." Sarah took Arminius' leash from Fritz and turned toward the Coiffure's front door.

"See you soon, Ms. Carter."

The tone of his voice reminded Sarah of Arnold Schwarzenegger's "I'll be back" in *The Terminator.* She didn't respond, but she opened the door and let Whiskey and Arminius in. Without looking back, she followed them inside.

Sarah removed Arminius' leash and instantly the tension that existed between Arminius and Whiskey lifted. They began playing, like young boys on the playground at recess, trying to prove who was stronger and faster.

"Wow, that's a gorgeous shepherd," said Emily.

"Yes, he is, but something isn't right about his human. He creeps me out." Sarah handed the white pastry bag to Emily, set her coffee tumbler on the counter, and looked at Fritz's business card.

Sarah read aloud, "Fritz von Falkenstein, President. International Solutions. Specializing in the priceless and valuable. Email: Fritz@internationalsolutions.com. Telephone: +49 30 5032 5358."

What does specializing in the priceless and valuable mean?

Extending her right arm and hand toward Emily and handing her the business card, Sarah said, "Before we get started on Arminius, could you look up this company?"

Emily took the card, pulled her laptop from her backpack, put it on the counter, and typed "International Solutions" into the search bar.

Sarah interrupted the dogs' wrestling. "Okay, boys. The fun is over for now. Arminius, you need to come with me. It's bath time." Sarah took Arminius back to the tub and began to fill it with warm water. Arminius looked at Whiskey, as if to say, "Is that for you or for me?"

Emily said, "I am not finding anything for this company. They do not have a web page or social media, and I can't find a thing about this von Frankenstein dude."

Sarah laughed. "I think its von Falkenstein."

"Whatever. It reminds me of looking for Mrs. Jenkins on the

web. I'd have better luck finding a flea on a black dog."

"Thanks for looking. Katie Smith should be arriving any minute with the sister Samoyeds Babs and Tabs."

Emily responded, "I am not sure who is prettier and well-groomed, Ms. Smith or Tabs and Babs?"

"Isn't that the truth," said Sarah. "All three of them have deep brown eyes that are so emotive."

"It's hard to believe that her husband divorced her. She seems like the perfect woman."

"Ginger told me that no one thought Katie would ever move back to Cottageville when she moved to the big city for undergrad then stayed for graduate school. According to Ginger, she was always a person with big dreams and going to make an impact on the world," said Sarah.

"That sucks."

The front door opened and in walked Katie, whose long, shiny black hair and alluring eyes made her look like she stepped off the cover of *Vogue.*

"Good morning, Ms. Colt," said Katie. "Here are my adorable girls, ready to be pampered for the day."

"Good morning, Ms. Smith. It's nice to see you and the sisters. We'll take good care of them. What color bows would you like today?" asked Emily.

"Let's go with red today. Thank you for asking. I have an appointment in fifteen minutes at Serene Escapes, so I will be in town. Please text me when the girls are ready."

"Will do," responded Emily.

"Thank you. I'll see you later." Katie hurried through the door.

Emily and Sarah stayed busy washing, grooming, and trimming nails all day. Arminius was exceptionally well behaved and mild mannered, which was a surprise to Sarah. Sarah figured with his behavior, self-control, and awareness, he had to be professionally trained.

Whiskey kept a watchful eye on the Samoyed sisters. He occasionally cocked his head at an angle, like he was questioning why they looked like twins.

As Emily and Sarah worked on Tabs and Babs, the front door opened. Whiskey, followed closely by Arminius, raced to the waiting area to welcome the next customer.

Squatting down to greet the two dogs, the chief said, "Good morning, Whiskey. Who is your friend?"

Both dogs licked the chief's neck and face and batted their paws at the chief's legs, trying to initiate a little roughhousing.

Feeling like Humpty Dumpty about to fall over, the chief stood to his feet and said, "Not today, guys. I have a lot of work to do."

Hearing the chief's voice, Sarah walked toward the counter. "Hey, Chief," said Sarah.

"Hello, Sarah. Whose beautiful shepherd is that?"

"His name is Arminius, and his human is a German guy named Fritz. Those are who I told you about early this morning. They are staying at the Whispering Pines. He gave me his business card, but it's weird, because Emily can't find him or the company online."

Chief Order scratched his chin. "You don't say. That is strange. I'll swing by the B&B and talked to the owners, Lisa and ... I can never remember her wife's name."

"Holly," said Sarah.

"Yes, Holly, that's her name. I will talk to Holly and Lisa and see if they have seen or heard anything odd about Fritz. Sarah, I made some calls after we talked this morning and was directed to the FBI. They have something called the Jewelry and Gem Theft Program, which works nationally and internationally with various law enforcement agencies to stop and capture jewelry thieves. I spoke to Director Mason, who, along with a handful of other agents, is boarding a plane in D.C. this evening and heading our way. They will arrive in Des Moines and visit the field office. Their plan is to spend the night in the city, then meet me at the station tomorrow mid-morning."

"Wow, Chief, our town is about to be put on the map," said Sarah.

Chief James chuckled. "Things are about to get interesting around here, that's for sure. I'll go talk to Holly and Lisa on my way back to the station. Thank you for making the connections you did."

"Thanks, Chief. And thanks for the heads up about the FBI."

"You bet, Sarah." The chief exited the Coiffure, crossed the street, and got into his cruiser. His mouth and speech seemed much better than the day before.

CHAPTER EIGHTEEN

Sarah adjusted Bab's bow. She thought that the vibrant red ribbon on the dogs gracefully contrasted with the Samoyed's pristine white fur. Whiskey and Arminius, both with heads cocked sideways, stood eying the sisters.

"I will text Ms. Smith and Fritz to let them know they can come by. Time for our lunch break."

Emily was enjoying the last bite of her delicious California wrap, filled with turkey, bacon, creamy avocado, and tomato, when Katie entered the Coiffure. Whiskey and Arminius, sprawled in opposite corners of the waiting room, lifted their heads to see who entered, but did not bother to greet the new guest.

Katie apologized for interrupting Emily's lunch.

Trying to talk and swallow at the same time, Emily mumbled that she was finished.

Sarah entered from the back room and asked Katie how the spa was.

"Wonderful. I even had time to enjoy a raspberry mocha with almond milk at Java and Juice afterward," Katie said. "I can't believe how many people have moved back to Cottageville. Each week I run into someone I knew when I was in elementary school. Like today, I talked to Jonathan Lake, a little chubby kid from my third-grade class. He's not little now, but he's still chubby!"

Sarah and Emily both snickered.

Katie continued, "People from other countries are moving here, too. At the café, I met this tall, very distinguished German man, who said he is moving here and is interested in buying Mrs. Jenkins' house. I didn't know her house was on the market."

Emily and Sarah both gasped. "Emily, he knew whose house it was," Sarah said under her breath.

Sarah changed the subject and talked to Katie about the spa's menu, while Emily retrieved the sisters. Tabs and Babs strode into the front room with the poise of seasoned show dogs, chests proudly raised, heads held high, and necks adorned with vibrant red bows that added an additional touch of elegance.

Squatting to their level, Katie, awed by her Samoyed's long, fluffy white fur and overall radiance, said, "My beautiful girls, look how adorable you are."

Emily and Sarah nodded their heads in agreement. Emily said,

"Yes, they are."

As Katie reached into her black leather crossbody purse to retrieve her credit card, the front door opened and in walked Fritz.

"Good afternoon, ladies. Katie, it's a pleasure to see you again, and so soon."

Katie's face turned various shades of red and she fumbled as she handed Emily her credit card. "Let me pay, and I will get out of your way so you can attend this man."

"Don't be ridiculous. I am in no rush. And here, allow me." Fritz handed Emily three crisp Benjamins. "Whatever is left, keep as a tip."

"No, no, I'm paying for—" Katie tried to talk, but Fritz cut her off mid-sentence.

"Look." Fritz pointed at the money in Emily's hand, "I already paid!"

Emily, not sure what to do, looked from Katie to Fritz. Fritz's eyes darkened and his face sported a scowl, so Emily returned the credit card to Katie.

Katie glared at him before putting her credit card in her wallet. "Thank you," she mumbled. She took the leashes from Emily, thanked Sarah and Emily, and led Babs and Tabs out the door and onto the street.

Arminius was no longer sprawled on the floor but was sitting as still and alert as a sphinx next to Fritz's left leg.

Fritz reached his hand into his front right pocket and pulled out a thick roll of one-hundred-dollar bills. "*Wie viel?*

"Pardon?" Emily. said

Fritz, laughing, repeated what he said, but this time in English.

"How much?"

"Oh," Emily said, frowning. "The full service, which includes brushing, hand wash, blow dry, ear cleaning, nail trimming, expressing anal glands, paw massage, and coat trim is $110."

Peeling two bills from the large roll, Fritz reached across the counter and handed them to Emily. "Here's two hundred; keep the rest."

Emily accepted the money and placed it in the cash drawer. "Thank you," she said.

Whiskey came over and nudged Arminius' neck with his cold wet nose, as if saying goodbye to his new friend.

Sarah spoke up and thanked Fritz for trusting them with Arminius and wished him well in his house-hunting and move to Cottageville. Fritz nodded, said, "*Danke*," and walked out the door with Arminius off his leash but staying close to his human's side.

"Man, Em, things are getting weird around here. How does Fritz know Mrs. Jenkins and why is he interested in her house? We need more clues, and we must find Mrs. Jenkins soon."

Emily agreed, as she looked down and scrolled on her phone.

"Emily, while you are on social media, could you see if anyone posted anything new in the Cottageville neighborhood group?"

"Sure." As she typed COTTAGEVILLE SOC the group popped up. Emily clicked on it and the page loaded. "There's only been one thing posted today at 9:57 a.m., and it's a poem."

"A poem? That's an odd thing to post in the group."

Emily agreed. "It's probably one of the old ladies in town that's bored and doesn't understand social media etiquette."

Sarah chuckled. "Is it any good?"

"Is what any good?

Laughing, Sarah said, "The poem, duh!"

Emily rolled her eyes, stood up straight, cleared her throat with an exaggerated sound, and began to read:

> *In shadows deep, where silence lies,*
>
> *an empty house, no echo cries.*
>
> *A sadden drunk lost in his thirst,*
>
> *vacant rooms where memories were accursed.*
>
> *A hostage held, in whispers cold,*
>
> *the truth untold, the tale unfolds.*
>
> *Guess the answer and set a liar free.*

"Emily, that sounds more like a riddle than a poem. Who posted it?"

"OMG," said Emily. "It's from NOONE!"

With a voice more appropriate for outside than in, Sarah said, "It must be a clue! Let's read it again."

Sarah stood behind Emily, looking over her left shoulder. The two of them read the riddle aloud in unison.

When they finished Sarah said, "Take a screen shot of the riddle and send it to the chief." She began to pace the floor in Coiffure's waiting room, going over the poem with each step. *In shadows deep, where silence lies. In the shadows deep. In the shadows deep, where silence lies. Where are the shadows? What shadows are deep?*

Emily picked her cell phone off the counter and answered it. "Hello, Chief. I am going to put you on speaker."

"Hi, Emily, I just got your text."

Sarah cut in, "Chief, this is a major clue. We need to decipher this riddle."

"It possibly could be. We need to show this to the FBI in the morning."

Sarah didn't like the sound of that. She wanted to solve the riddle. She didn't need cocky dudes with badges and fancy titles to solve Cottageville's mystery. They were perfectly capable of doing it themselves. Now irritated and feeling anxious, Sarah let out a big "ugh!"

"You okay, Sarah?" inquired the chief.

"I'm frustrated. There are so many clues and pieces to this that we must start putting them together if we are going to find Mrs. Jenkins."

Emily piped in, "Speaking of clues, we found out today from Katie Smith that Fritz wants to buy Mrs. Jenkins' house. Meaning that when Sarah ran into him on the sidewalk, he already knew whose house it was when he said he thought it was abandoned and he was snooping around."

The chief interjected as Emily finished her sentence, "Speaking of Fritz, Holly took the day off, so I spoke with Lisa at the Whispering Pines. She said that Fritz is extremely friendly, very professional, and talks to everyone. The only unusual behavior she mentioned was that Fritz paid his week's stay in cash, up front at the time of check in. Two-thousand four-hundred and fifty dollars in crisp one-hundred-dollar bills, and he didn't want back the fifty dollars in change but said to have dinner on him."

Sarah's voice was tight when she said, "It's odd not to use a credit card, but I don't see anything suspicious. And we have seen today that he is very generous. Maybe where he's from in Germany they like cash and don't like to use credit cards."

"Or maybe we need to check the Benjamins he paid with today because they might be counterfeit," remarked Emily. She pulled out the special marker they had to check bills and opened the drawer and scribbled on the bills, as Sarah said, "Great! Now we might have a jewel thief, a counterfeiter, and a kidnapper?"

Laughing at Sarah, Emily said, "Don't forget about car thieves and a graffiti artist."

The chief chuckled and said, "You forgot burglar and jay walker."

They laughed and as they heard the others' laughs, they laughed even more. It was one of those contagious moments, when you no longer laugh at what was said, but you laugh because you are laughing,

When Emily stopped, she said, "Our bills are good."

"So maybe not a counterfeiter," the chief said.

"I guess not," Emily said.

The front door opened and in walked Jared. "Holy cow, are you both stoned? What am I missing?"

Trying to pull herself together, Sarah said, "Aren't you supposed to be at work?"

Jared was quick with a response. "Yes. I ran an iced caramel latte to Addison a few doors down and so I figured I'd stop and say hello. Obviously, I missed something though."

Whiskey walked over to greet his buddy, so Jared reached down and scratched under Whiskey's chin. The more Jared scratched, the more Whiskey made noises of enjoyment. "Tell me what's going on. What did I miss?"

Emily said, "The chief's on the phone here."

"Hi, Chief," Jared said.

"Hi, Jared."

Then Sarah told Jared about Katie and her comments about Fritz wanting to buy Mrs. Jenkins' house, Fritz bringing Arminius to the Coiffure, and how they just saw the post from NOONE on the Cottageville social media group.

"Wow, this is all crazy. Can I see the riddle? Did you figure any of it out?" asked Jared.

Similar to earlier, Emily stood up straight and proper, like she was reading official documents in a courtroom and read:

> In shadows deep, where silence lies,
>
> an empty house, no echo cries.
>
> A sadden drunk lost in his thirst,
>
> vacant rooms where memories were accursed.
>
> A hostage held, in whispers cold,
>
> the truth untold, the tale unfolds.
>
> Guess the answer and set a liar free.

"Someone put a lot of time and thought into this riddle," said Jared.

Sarah agreed and started to repeat the riddle, expecting the neural pathways in her brain to connect and bring forth revelation.

Emily spoke up, "At least we know there is an empty house."

"Well, that's our first clue in solving the riddle, an empty house," said the chief.

Jared said, "An empty house, no echo cries. That sounds like since the house is empty, you can't hear crying."

"But if the house is empty, there would be an echo because nothing absorbs the sound," reasoned the chief.

"Let's look at the first part. Maybe it relates to the empty house with no echo," said Sarah.

The chief and the three wanna-be detectives pondered the first line over and over. They felt like they were so close to understanding it, but the answers kept eluding them.

Whiskey pawed at the front door and woofed. "What is it, boy?" Sarah asked.

Emily said, "I don't think he's been out since this morning."

Sarah walked over to the door, pushed it open, and stepped outside, where Whiskey lifted his leg and released a solid stream onto the grass between the sidewalk and the street. "Good boy, Whiskey! Let's go back inside."

As Sarah walked back into the building, Jared enthused, "I think I got it. *In shadows deep, where silence lies, an empty house, no echo cries.* The silence is already there, that's why no echo cries. Meaning there is silence, so you won't hear an echo. If I am correct, there is an empty house somewhere where there is silence."

The chief agreed with Jared. "It appears to say there is a house somewhere it's so quiet you can't even hear an echo. But what's shadow's deep?"

Emily quickly answered, "Give me two seconds more. Got it.

I asked AI on my phone app what is *In shadows deep, where silence lies* and, are you ready for this? It said it could be referring to a forest, where it is silent from the developed world and the tall trees cast shadows deep into the forest."

"Oh, my goodness," said Sarah. 'Let's put it all together now. There is an empty house, deep enough in the woods that from the house, you can't hear anything but silence."

"Yes," Jared said, "that sounds right."

"That's brilliant," Chief Order said. "Good work."

Sarah, Emily, and Jared celebrated their small victory and gave each other high fives, like they had just scored the tie-breaking goal in the Stanley Cup playoffs. Whiskey sat on his haunches and lifted his front paw to high five with them, too. He gave one sharp bark.

"Well done, Whiskey," Chief Order said over the speakerphone, before he laughed.

The chief told the group that he needed to take care of things at the station before the FBI arrived in the morning. He encouraged the amateur detectives to continue working on the riddle and to refrain from sharing too much information with people outside of their circle.

Jared told Sarah he'd catch up with her later and went back to Java and Juice to finish his shift. Emily and Sarah continued attending to their fluffy and furry clients until they were finally able to call it a day.

CHAPTER NINETEEN

At nine a.m. sharp, three black SUVs, with dark tinted windows—too dark to be legal for a civilian vehicle in the Midwest—and official government plates rolled up and parked in front of Carter's Canine Coiffure. Four men exited from each vehicle in a way that said they meant business. Like in the movies, they wore black pants, white laundered dress shirts, black ties, and standard-issue blue jackets with the letters FBI in yellow. Two agents positioned themselves on opposite sides of their respective vehicles, two others took up spots on the opposite corners of the block, two took posts at the front door of the Coiffure, and two entered the shop.

As they walked through the green door, Emily lifted her head and Whiskey bolted to the front room to welcome the new guests. Sarah was busy refilling the shampoo and conditioner bottles. She looked at the waiting room, unsure why the men were there.

"Good morning, miss. My name is Director Mason. I am with a special task force from the Jewelry and Gem Theft Program of the FBI."

"Hello, Director Mason. My name is Sarah Carter, that friendly fella is Whiskey, and this is Emily Colt. It's a pleasure to meet you."

They shook hands, and then the director introduced the gentleman on his right. "Ladies, this is Special Agent Lee. He is one of the finest agents I have ever worked with. Together, with the rest of our agents and your help, we are going to find Mrs. Jenkins and solve this crime."

"Wonderful," replied Sarah. "We sure hope that Mrs. Jenkins is okay."

Looking directly into Sarah's eyes with eyes that held no expression and with a stone face, the director told Sarah that he believed Mrs. Jenkins was unharmed, because the people who abducted her were thieves and not murderers.

Mason continued, "Ladies, I am not sure what you know about Mrs. Jenkins, but I assure you, she's not who you think she is."

Sarah raised her eyebrows and cocked her head to the side, like a dog that heard an unfamiliar sound. She asked the director what he meant.

"I am not at liberty to divulge details, but you will discover the truth soon enough. Now, if you will excuse me for a moment, I need to step outside and make a call. Special Agent Lee will take over from here."

Whiskey followed Director Mason to the door but remained inside. Special Agent Lee, a no-nonsense, forty-something-year-old man, had jet black hair and a traditional military buzz cut. By his actions and demeanor, he resembled a special forces character in a movie. His chiseled face and body screamed, "I can kill you if I need to." Sarah shuddered when she thought that.

Special Agent Lee removed some photos from his inner jacket pocket and strategically placed the pictures on the counter.

"Where did you get those pictures?" asked Sarah.

With a look of disgust, Agent Lee responded, "We are the FBI, Ms. Carter."

Under her breath, Sarah mumbled, "Jerk."

"Here are the pictures of the jewelry that you found in Cottageville. Chief Order sent them to us yesterday. Here are other pictures that we have accumulated over the years, along with a picture of the museum where they were stolen."

Emily interjected, "We saw on the internet that they were stolen from the Pforzheim Jewelry Museum."

"That is correct, Ms. Colt. Except for these items." Lee pointed to three of the pictures. "This gold bangle bracelet, the pair of earrings shaped like Irish claddagh, and the thick ouroboros. These items were stolen twenty-two years ago from The Museum of Jewellery in the Via de la Plata, Spain."

Sarah, lighting up like a Christmas tree, exclaimed, "No way! We found jewelry in Cottageville that was stolen from two different famous museums?"

Agent Lee, slightly less intense now, said, "That is correct, Ms. Carter."

Still on the phone talking, Director Mason returned through Coiffure's front door. Looking toward Sarah, he said, "Chief Order tells me you have a riddle you are trying to solve. Can we see it, please?"

Emily reached into the back right pant pocket of her black and white checkered bell bottoms and removed her phone. Pulling up the Cottageville social media group, she placed her phone on the counter for the two men to see.

"Okay. Thanks, Chief Order. We will see you in a little while," said the director before he disconnected the call.

Reading aloud, but not loud enough that all could hear him clearly, the director said:

In shadows deep, where silence lies,

an empty house, no echo cries.

A sadden drunk lost in his thirst,

vacant rooms where memories were accursed.

A hostage held, in whispers cold,

the truth untold, the tale unfolds.

Guess the answer and set a liar free.

As the director finished saying *....and set a liar free,* Emily interjected, "This is what we deciphered so far, there is an empty house, deep enough in the woods that from the house, you can't hear anything but silence."

Special Agent Lee, whose countenance no longer resembled a Doberman pinscher on watch, said, "Very impressive work, Emily."

"Teamwork, sir. Jared, Sarah, the chief, and I worked on it last night."

"Good job, ladies," said Director Mason. "Lee, can you and Emily work on deciphering more of the riddle? Sarah, I need you to walk me through the timeline of events, starting with the first day you discovered something was wrong and ending with last night and the riddle."

Emily and Special Agent Lee stood across from each other at the counter, while Sarah and Director Mason moved to the far end, talking through the details from Sarah's perspective.

As Sarah shared the information with the director, she realized how enthralled she was with this mystery. It was more than simply finding Mrs. Jenkins, she discovered a passion being stirred to dive deeper, to pay attention to details, and in some ways, to prove to herself that she could solve this crime.

"Director Mason, sir. Sorry to interrupt, but I believe we have another clue," said Special Agent Lee. He turned toward Emily, "Emily, please read it."

Emily read, "A sadden drunk lost in his thirst, vacant rooms where memories were accursed."

"Sir, Emily and I believe that something bad happened in the house, something that caused a person to become a drunk."

Excited like Sam the affenpinscher she had groomed last week, Emily squealed, "When you put these parts together it sounds like something tragic happened in a house deep in the woods, which caused someone to become a drunk and abandon the house."

Alarms went off in Sarah's mind. Her attention turned quickly to her colleague. "Em, read the next part."

Emily began, "A hostage held, in whispers cold, the truth untold, the tale unfolds. Guess the answer and set a liar free."

Sarah slammed her hand down on the counter to say she solved the riddle. "Mrs. Jenkins is being held captive in an abandoned house deep in the woods. Remember, whoever is behind this called Mrs. Jenkins a liar. The riddle says, if we find the hostage held, which is Mrs. Jenkins, then the truth will be discovered and the liar, supposedly Mrs. Jenkins, will be rescued, or freed."

As Sarah finished explaining the riddle, an agent cracked the door open enough to show his face but shield the view from the outside with his body and said, "Director, sir, there is an Officer James Order here to speak with you."

"Let him in, Remington."

"Good morning. Nice to meet you," said the chief, extending his right hand toward Director Mason.

The two shook, and then the director introduced the chief to Lee. After their brief formalities, the director turned to Sarah and motioned for her to tell the chief about the latest discoveries.

"Chief, the riddle says that Mrs. Jenkin's is being held hostage in an abandoned house deep within the woods, a house where something tragic happened and someone became a drunk. Also, when we find Mrs. Jenkins, we will know the truth."

The Chief smirked and shook his head. "You never cease to amaze me!"

Special Agent Lee, back in military mode, told the director that he was going out to the truck to call and have satellite images of the surrounding areas sent to their government-issued tablets.

"Chief Order, how well do you know Cottageville?" asked the director.

"Really well. I have lived here my entire life."

"We will have satellite images sent to us within the next hour or so, but in the meantime, can you think of any possible areas where this abandoned house deep in the woods might be?"

Before the chief could answer, Lee entered through the front door and told the director that the images would be sent soon. He also informed Sarah and Emily that the agents on the sidewalk are with a man and two shelties that said they had an appointment at 9:30 a.m.

"Oh, that's right. He texted they rolled in something," responded Emily. "What should we do?"

Looking at his watch, then at Lee, the director told Emily and Sarah that they should attend to their customers and work a normal day, unless something transpired after they received the satellite images.

Sarah, not wanting to miss out, suggested that Emily stay and run things, and since it was going to be a slow day, she and Whiskey would go and assist the FBI.

"Okay. That sounds good," responded the director.

Looking toward Emily, Sarah asked her if she was going to be okay without her help. Emily assured her she'd be fine.

The federal agents at the door escorted Sergio, Sebastian, and Sophie into the Coiffure. Whiskey was thrilled to see the shelties. With his tail wagging, he gave them a two-woof welcome and circled around them with his herding instincts, and they tried to herd him right back.

"Ladies, what in the world is going on around here? It's easier to get into the White House than it is to Carter's Canine Coiffure."

Everyone laughed at Sergio's comment. Emily received Sergio's shelties and explained briefly that the FBI came to assist in finding Mrs. Jenkins. As Emily and Sergio talked, Sarah and Whiskey left the shop, along with Special Agent Lee, the chief, and Director Mason.

Sarah thought, *this is really happening. The FBI is here in Cottageville. As much as I didn't want them here, this is cool. Forget Nancy Drew or even Angela Lansbury in* Murder, She Wrote, *I am working with the FBI. This is next level stuff.*

"Sarah, have you given any thought to where this abandoned house might be?" asked the chief.

He received no response as Sarah was still daydreaming.

"Sarah?" asked the chief again.

"What? I am sorry, Chief. What did you ask?"

"I wondered if you thought of any parts of Cottageville where this abandoned house might be."

"That's a good question. Off the top of my head, I'd say either at the far east part of town beyond the river, or the far west part of town, in the portion just before you leave our town limits. That wooded area goes for miles way up into the hills."

The chief, trying to visualize those areas of town, said, "With that much land to cover, we better wait for the satellite images before we head out."

"Yes," responded Director Mason. "We will wait for the images. They will save us a lot of time and energy." Looking at his watch again, the Director inquired of a place for them all to go get coffee.

Sarah answered quickly, "The best place in town would be Java and Juice. We can walk there."

Special Agent Lee, Director Mason, the chief, Sarah, and Whiskey walked toward Java and Juice, while the rest of the agents remained in their positions by the vehicles, in front of the Coiffure, and on the corners of the block. Along the way, Whiskey greeted various townspeople, but the humans were lost in their thoughts.

A hush came over Java and Juice as the crew entered through the painted red door. It was an eerie quiet, like the moment before something happens in a horror movie. Whiskey made his way over to the counter to greet Jared while everyone else got into line to order. From behind the counter, on the far left, Ginger, with her curly blond hair pulled tightly back and tied with a rubber band, waved to Sarah and the chief.

"This looks like a nice, quaint place, " said the Director.

"Yes, my best friend, who just greeted us, owns it. Just wait until you try their coffee. It's to die for. And, they have amazing homemade pastries that will dance on your taste buds."

Chuckling, the Director said, "Wow, are the pastries a symphony of delectable flavors as well?"

Sarah wasn't sure how to respond. *Was he being sarcastic?*

Chief Order chuckled.

Only a few minutes passed, and they were up next to order. "Hello gentlemen, what can I get for you today?" asked Jared.

"Hey, there is a lady with us," said Agent Lee.

"That's not a lady," responded Jared. "That's mi 'lady!'"

Sarah laughed and took a little dip. "Good day, my lord!"

Jared grinned and said to Special Agent Lee that he already

knew Sarah's order.

Agent Lee mumbled, "Small town living."

Director Mason ordered a twenty-ounce oat milk latte and an apple tart. Special Agent Lee ordered a double shot espresso, and following a Paleo diet, asked for the almond flour lemon-raspberry scone, and Chief Order ordered a twelve-ounce dark roast and a cinnamon and brown sugar croissant. The band of sleuths stepped to the right side of the counter to wait for Jared and Ginger to fulfill their order. As they were waiting, Fritz entered Java and Juice with Arminius. Whiskey was elated. The two dogs greeted each other with affectionate nudges and ear nibbling.

The Director took his eyes off the large German shepherd playing with Whiskey and glanced up at the tall, distinguished man that entered the cafe. He exclaimed, "Fritz! What in the—?"

With an element of surprise in her voice Sarah questioned, "Excuse me, you know him?"

"Know him? Fritz and I go way back. We've worked on cases around the world together for the past twenty-five years."

After walking to them, Fritz wrapped his large wingspan of arms around Director Mason and said, "*dich zu sehen, alter Freund.*"

"It's good to see you too, Fritz!"

The two laughed, released their embrace, and walked toward a table in the front of the cafe, close to the bay window. Arminius stayed with Whiskey, now both seated next to where Sarah stood. She raised her eyebrows at Chief Order.

The Director and Fritz sat down across from one another. "Fritz, old friend, I've gotta ask you. What are you doing here in Cottageville, and why didn't I know you were coming?"

Fritz, with a mischievous smirk, said, "You know how these things work, Mase. I must do what I am told. Besides..." He laughed a little. "I knew we'd end up at the same place on this case."

Director Mason smiled at Fritz. "You've always been a bit mysterious, and you seem to show up at the right place at the right time and are often a step or two ahead of us."

Fritz grinned. "It's German logic!"

They both laughed and welcomed Lee, Sarah, and the chief as they delivered the Director's oat milk latte and apple tart puff. Fritz encouraged them to pull up some chairs and join their conversation.

Crowded around the small bistro table by the bay window, they all leaned in and listened intently as Fritz began to speak. Even Whiskey seemed interested in the conversation as he sat at attention next to Arminius, who seemed to tower over him, like an elephant seal next to a sea lion.

CHAPTER TWENTY

As the group sat huddled together around the table, they looked like a football squad discussing the next play before breaking to take their positions at the line of scrimmage. Fritz, in a soft, yet commanding voice, explained to Director Mason that he was unable to make known his travels to Cottageville and his assignment because their intelligence revealed that the FBI was compromised and someone on the inside had been working with Mrs. Jenkins over the years.

"Wait, what?" uttered Sarah.

Fritz stared at Director Mason. "Would you like to explain, Mase?"

"Um, hmm, let me think for a moment." Looking out the bay window, as if the elements outside were going to magically bring clarity, he said, "How can I explain, but keep things confidential?"

Laughing, Fritz quipped, "I can tell them if you'd like, considering our jurisdictions are different."

"That's not a bad idea, Fritz. Thank you for that."

Despite the conversations in the cafe, the sound of the espresso machine, and orders being called, the only sound Sarah could hear was the sound of Fritz's voice. Fritz slowly turned his head, making eye contact with each person at the table. "I will not go into detail, but simply tell you the facts. Mrs. Jenkins was a Special Agent with the FBI. She was, from what I know, one of the best trained agents the Bureau had recruited. She is brilliant, speaks a minimum of five languages fluently, and is a nice person, too. Many years ago, she and her husband, a special undercover agent from France, were on a joint operation commissioned by, umm, never mind who commissioned it. They, along with many other agents from France, Germany, Spain, Italy, and the U.S. infiltrated the largest stolen art and jewelry ring in the world. They were about to bust things wide open, but things went sideways. There were people high up in the government from the countries involved in the sting and those people were making millions by overlooking the corruption and making crimes disappear. They turned the agents' names over to the underground world, and one by one, the group of international agents assigned to the task force were assassinated. And I don't mean simply shot, but beheaded, sawed in half, and blown up. Each assassination was gruesome and was meant to send a message. Mrs. Jenkins' husband Marquis, was captured in

Austria, tortured, then burned alive. June, or Mrs. Jenkins as you know her, managed to disappear and has not been seen or heard from since. Well, not until recently when dark web chatter mentioned that she was located here in Cottageville."

Sarah and the chief stared intently at Fritz, then shifted their eyes to Director Mason, as a way of asking if what Fritz was saying was true.

Acknowledging their inquisitive looks, the Director picked up where Fritz stopped. "Mrs. Jenkins, speaking multiple languages and having many aliases and passports, managed to travel from country to country, seeking to avenge her husband's death and the death of fellow agents. Being brilliant, she devised a plan. Instead of targeting the organizations contracted to kill the agents, June went to the source. Through her contacts and informants, she discovered which countries were lining their pockets through trafficking and which governments okayed the hit. Then, what she did next was ingenious. She robbed each country's most recognized museums of their precious and priceless jewelry collections."

"But why jewelry from museums?" asked the chief. "That seems like an odd thing to steal to punish a country."

"That's the beauty of it," said Fritz. "Remember, in Old World countries, history, the arts, and culture mean everything. It is not like the United States where everyone wants new and modern. Countries that have large museums, full of heirlooms, artwork, jewelry, and artifacts are considered powerful and wealthy. Also, museums in some of these countries are known for trafficking and fencing stolen goods. With the government's blind eye, many museums are directly involved with the very trafficking ring that Mrs. Jenkins infiltrated. By stealing jewelry from these museums, she sent messages to the underground world that the museums were no longer a safe place for them to traffic goods, which ultimately hurt the museums' profits and the government officials that were getting rich."

"I gotta ask, is Mrs. Jenkins good or bad? Cause I think I am cheering for her," said Sarah. "It's like how I cheered for Dominic Toretto in *Fast and the Furious*, even though he was a criminal."

Director Mason smiled, "Mrs. Jenkins is a good person, Sarah. However, a crime is a crime anyway you look at it. Life doesn't turn out like the movies where a good person who does bad things is pardoned because of good intentions. Mrs. Jenkins broke international laws, trafficked stolen goods, and used her government clearance to conduct illegal activity."

Cracking a smile beneath his silver beard and looking into Sarah's eyes, Fritz said, "Sarah, Mrs. Jenkins is a good human and she's the good guy in my eyes."

A warmth came over Sarah. She had always been a good judge of character and knew deep inside that Mrs. Jenkin's wasn't a bad person.

Looking over the table at Fritz, Director Mason leaned in and asked him to tell him what information he had regarding the possibility of a corrupt agent within the FBI. Fritz explained that someone within the Bureau had been removing any footprints that June might have left.

"So, they weren't involved in the crimes but have been involved in keeping Mrs. Jenkins' whereabouts and real identity a secret?" said the Director.

"From the intelligence that we have gathered, that is correct."

"Wow," said Sarah, "Mrs. Jenkins has been on the run all these years and has had help from someone on the inside, yet here you are in Cottageville, about to find her. This is exciting but I am sad too. I really like Mrs. Jenkins; I can't imagine her spending the rest of her life in a prison in a foreign country. That would be awful."

Agent Lee interrupted, "Director Mason, sir, I just received a text from Agent Johnson. The satellite images are now streaming to our tablets."

"Thank you, Agent Lee. Let's head back to the vehicles and make a search and rescue plan. Fritz, are joining us on this?"

"Absolutely," Fritz said, with a contagious smile, "as long as no one knows we are working together."

"It might be too late for that." But as Director Mason stood up from the table, he smiled at Fritz. "As they say, what happens in America, stays in America."

They all chuckled, returned their chairs to the appropriate tables, and started making their way to the front door. Sarah scooted over to the counter and had a brief dialogue with Jared and Ginger. "I will keep you posted. Text me when you get off work." Whiskey and Arminius led the way down the sidewalk to the front of Carter's Canine Coiffure. The agents were ready with the government-issued tablets in hand, eager to pass them to Director Mason and Agent Lee.

"Thank you, gentlemen," said the Director, as he took the tablet from Agent Johnson.

Agent Johnson handed Agent Lee his tablet and, pointing with his left index finger at the screen, said, "We've already highlighted two areas that are secluded and show some form of building in the image."

With the tablets now resting on the hood of the first black SUV in the line of three, everyone gathered around to view the satellite images.

Taking charge, Director Mason, looking at the time on the tablet, said, "It's one-one-zero-five hours, so we still have plenty of daylight. We are going to split into two teams. Team one will go to the east side of town beyond the river. Team two will start in the west part of town, but in here." He put his finger on the screen and said, "in the portion just before the town limits."

Stepping back away from the SUV for a moment, Director Mason put his hands up over his head, grasping his left hand with his right. He stood up on his toes and stretched his whole body toward the sky. As he came off his toes and dropped his arms, he ordered Lee to divide up the teams.

"Yes, sir. Team one will be Johnson, Remington, Jones, Martinez, Fox, and myself. Team one will head east. Team two will be Director Mason, Schultz, Hussain, McArthur, Henderson, and Miles. Team two will head west. Chief Order, I am assigning you and Fritz to team two, with the director. If you, plus Arminius, could follow team two in your cruiser, that would be appreciated. Team one, divide up between the two lead SUVs. Team two, load up in the last SUV, but Miles, go with the chief in the cruiser."

"Everyone understand?" asked Director Mason. "Stay on your coms and stay alert. Let's roll."

Scrambling to their designated vehicles, everyone seemed anxious to get on the road. Miles looked uncomfortable as he made his way to the cruiser, opened the back passenger door, and crawled into the back seat.

Sarah's eyes were wide, and she was itching to get into a vehicle. "What about me? Who do I ride with?"

Director Mason turned toward Sarah, "This is official government business. Civilians are not allowed."

Feeling like a small sailboat that lost the driving force of the wind, Sarah dropped her head and walked toward the green door of the Coiffure. Whiskey, sensing Sarah's disappointment, mirrored her body language and followed at her side. *This isn't fair,* she thought.

Fritz opened the back driver side door of the cruiser and in response to his German command, Arminius jumped in the back with Agent Miles.

Fritz leaned down to make eye contact with Agent Miles. "I hope you like big dogs."

Miles smiled and scratched behind Arminius' ears. Arminius, with his monster-sized body, sprawled out across the seat, with his head on Agent Miles' lap.

Chief Order and Fritz climbed into the front seat of the cruiser simultaneously. "Are you guys ready?" asked the chief.

"Yes, sir," Agent Miles replied. "However, I must admit, this is my first time in the back of a police car and I'm hoping it's the last."

The chief laughed, then added, "In my experience, if you've made it into the back seat of a police cruiser once, chances are you will be there again in the future."

"Wonderful." Agent Miles rolled his eyes and looked out the window, watching Sarah and Whiskey as they entered her shop.

The cruiser moved forward and fell in line behind black SUV number three.

Agent Miles noticed the chief's knuckles were a bit white as he gripped the steering wheel. He heard him take an audible breath in before he said, "Here we go."

Fritz and Chief Order talked about handguns and their favorite grain of ammo, while Agent Miles scratched Arminius' ears and looked out the window. As their small caravan came to the cross section of Grant Street and Route Nine, the lead SUVs made a right onto Route Nine, while the third SUV and police cruiser made a left and headed west.

Sarah and Whiskey entered the Coiffure, and with the sound of the bell, Emily yelled from the back, "I'll be right with you."

"It's okay, Em. It's just us." Sarah passed the counter and entered the area where Emily was blow-drying Sophie. "How's it going?"

Emily 's voice carried over the handheld blow-dryer's hum. "Fine. Sophie and Sebastian are chill."

Whiskey greeted Sebastian and Sophie, then returned to the front door and sat anxiously waiting, like a small child awaiting the arrival of his parents at the end of a workday.

"Sarah, I didn't expect to see you back here today."

"I didn't either. But Director Mason informed me that civilians have no place in official government business."

"That sucks. Does he not realize that we are the ones who have been solving this mystery?

"Yeah, but policy is policy."

Turning off the blow-dryer, Emily said, "Sarah, you aren't quitting, are you? You can't give up now that we are so close to solving this and saving Mrs. Jenkins."

Looking as if she had just received a shot from an EpiPen, Sarah was buzzing with life again.

"You are right. Emily. The Director said I couldn't go with them, but he never told me to stand down." Smiling at Emily, she added, "Would Lara Croft give up if a government official told her to?"

"Heck no!"

"I need to find out who owns property in the areas the two teams are going to. Would you be okay if I ran across town to the county clerk's office? Maybe the recorder of deeds is available, or at least someone there could point me in the right direction."

Emily grinned. "I got this Sarah, and I am looking forward to my raise after this is all done!"

"You got it, Em. It is time, and you deserve one." Heading out of the grooming area, Sarah told Whiskey they were leaving. At that, he perked up and circled twice in front of the door.

Arriving at the country clerk's office, Sarah introduced herself to Martha, and asked to see the recorder of deeds. Martha, a seventy-six-year-old widow, with a silver beehive, smiled big at Sarah.

"I'm sorry, dear, but Mr. Watson is on vacation until next Thursday. Is there anything I can help you with?"

"Martha, is there any way I could see an aerial map of Cottageville? And is there a way to see who owns property in the far east and far west parts of town?"

"Young lady, that's an odd request. Could you be a little more specific, so I know where to send you for help?"

Sarah struggled for a few moments before she could articulate what she wanted without sounding totally crazy. Since the townspeople were keeping up with Mrs. Jenkins' disappearance, Sarah gave Martha a recap of the latest discoveries, then came straight out and said, "I need to know who owns houses on the far east side of town beyond the river and the far west side of town, before the town limits."

"Let's start with the easy one. I have lived here my entire life and have worked in this same department for forty-four years, so I pretty much know this town like the back of my hand. In the west region you are referring to, there aren't too many property owners or houses. In fact, since the seventies, it's been prohibited to buy land there. The county wants to preserve that last part of the forest that remains in Cottageville. A parcel of land could only be passed down from generation to generation, and most of the new generation wanted to move closer to the city, so they sold out to the county."

"What records can I look through to see who still owns land there?" Sarah asked Martha.

With a smirk and funny laugh, "Honey, did I not tell you that I know everything about Cottageville? I've lived here my entire life. I will tell you, there's no need for you to be digging through archives."

Sarah stared at Martha for beat and thought, *I feel like this is a scene from a TV series.*

Martha interrupted her thought. "I can only think of three families that still have property in this area, the Livingstons, the Millers, and Bunky Buffalo was left with the house after his mother passed."

Sarah straightened her posture as enlightened descended. She gasped and that got Whiskey's attention. "That's it! That's the person in the riddle. *A sadden drunk lost in his thirst,* that sadden drunk is Bunky Buffalo."

"What?"

"I think I just solved the riddle," replied Sarah. "Bunky became a drunk when his mother died, was arrested when he shot things up, and has been in jail ever since, leaving his house abandoned in the woods."

"I am totally lost," said Martha.

"I am sorry, Martha, but I gotta run. Thank you so much for your help. Let's go, Whiskey." Running out of the county clerk's office, like she was running the last leg of a 1,600 meter, four-person team relay, Sarah and Whiskey made it back to Carter's Canine Coiffure in no time at all.

CHAPTER TWENTY-ONE

arah and Whiskey bursting through green door caused Travis and Emily both jumped in startlement. Even the shelties gave a nervous whimper. "OMG, Sarah, you just gave me a heart attack," said Em.

"Bunky Buffalo! It's Bunky Buffalo's house."

"What's Bunky Buffalo?"

"Emily, he's the answer to the riddle. He's the one who became a drunk; Mrs. Jenkins is being held in his abandoned house. I guarantee it."

As Whiskey nudged Sebastian and Sophie, Travis stood silent and baffled. "Guys, what did I miss?"

"Sorry, Travis, but I don't have time to explain. Emily, put the closed sign on the door and come with me. Let's run to my house and get my Jeep. We can call the chief on the way. Sorry, Travis, we gotta go."

"Ah, um, okay," Travis awkwardly mumbled. "I guess I'll see you around, Emily."

They quickly ushered Travis, Sebastian, and Sophie out the front door. Exiting through the door as well, Sarah pulled the door shut and locked it and headed down the sidewalk with Emily and Whiskey.

Sarah and Whiskey usually stopped and talked to people, but not today. The three sleuths were on a mission, there was not time to stop.

"Sarah, the next time you decide to take me running, remind me not to wear platform Vans."

Barely able to laugh because of shortness of breath, Sarah said, "I don't know how you do anything in those shoes."

"I do what I am supposed to in them, I look hot."

Whiskey, with tongue hanging out the left side of his mouth, must have liked Emily's response, because he timed two woofs perfectly.

As they made it to Sarah's property line she said, "Finally. I don't think I could run any further."

"M-yyy legs are shaking, and I think my heart is about to explode."

"Put your hands up on your head while I go in and grab the keys."

Emily walked down the driveway toward Sarah's vintage kelly green 1969 Jeep CJ5. Sarah's grandfather restored the CJ and gave it to

Sarah for her sixteen birthday. Shortly afterward, he passed away from pancreatic cancer, so Sarah kept it immaculate, seldom drove it, and vowed to never part with it.

Sarah returned in a few seconds and tossed an ice-cold bottle of spring water to Emily, then unlocked the driver's side door, which unlocked the passenger door. "Jump in, Whiskey," Sarah said.

Turning the key to the ignition, the CJ5's 225ci dauntless V6 turned over like it was a brand-new motor. Putting in the clutch, Sarah slid the three-speed transmission into reverse and headed backwards down the driveway. Out on the road, she gracefully went from reverse to first with the precision of an experienced stockcar driver.

"Route Nine West, here we come," said Sarah. "Can you call the chief?"

Emily reached into her right front pants pocket and struggled a bit to retrieve her phone, but after a little wiggling in the seat, she managed to take her phone out but couldn't find the chief's number in her contacts.

"Sarah, I need to call from your phone. I don't have the chief's number."

Reaching down with her left hand, Emily grabbed Sarah's phone off of the seat next to Sarah's right hip. Knowing Sarah's password, Emily unlocked Sarah's phone and scrolled until she found the chief's number. Hitting the call button, Emily sat listening for the phone to ring.

"It's not ringing, Sarah."

Taking her eyes off the road for a brief second and looking at Emily, Sarah said, "I wonder if they are driving through the valley on

Route Nine. The signal there is terrible."

"I will try again in a few minutes."

They drove for five minutes in silence before Sarah said, "Em, try the chief again."

"I have, but it goes straight to his voicemail."

"Man, we've gotta get a hold of him. If not, they will be searching for hours out there."

"Can you please text Jared and Ginger and tell them where we are going? At least someone will know where we are is something crazy happens."

"What do you mean if something crazy happens, Sarah?"

"I'm just saying, we don't know if we will get a hold the chief before we get there, and who knows what will happen when we get to Bunky's house?"

"You aren't thinking about us going there alone, are you?

With a huge grin, Sarah turned toward Emily. "We aren't alone, we have each other, and most importantly, we have Whiskey."

Whiskey's ears perked up and he gave a low growl.

Emily sent a group text to Ginger and Jared, which read, "This is Emily, Sarah and I are enroute to Bunky Buffalo's house. Sarah solved the riddle and is certain that Mrs. Jenkins is being held hostage there. Chief Order's phone is out of range. If you don't hear from us again, call the police. (joke, no joke)."

For the next ten minutes, the only sound was the hum of the oversized Jeep tires on the road. Sarah imagined possible scenarios as she drove, including a dramatic rescue, Whiskey tackling a bag guy, her cutting Mrs. Jenkins free from a chair in the corner of a dark room and running to safety.

"We are getting close to the turn off, Emily. Try the chief again."

"Still nothing, Sarah. What are we going to do?"

"Hopefully we will find the guys when we pull off of Route Nine and onto the dirt road."

"I sure hope so."

Putting her turn signal on, Sarah downshifted, and began to slow the Jeep down before turning left off of Route Nine and onto the dirt route that would eventually lead to Bunky's abandoned house.

Emily's eyes shifted from the sides of the road to the road ahead and back again. "I don't see the Black SUVs or the chief's cruiser."

"They probably started following the dirt road up into the back country. Everything is going to be okay."

A half-mile down the dirt road, Sarah, Whiskey, and Emily drove up a steep incline that eventually leveled off. They traveled another tenth of a mile and came upon a sharp series of s curves through dense thickets of trees. Coming out the last s curve, they spied, parked in an open field on the right side of the road, were one Black SUV and the chief's cruiser.

"There they are, Sarah!"

Pulling up behind the cruiser, Sarah said, "The cars are here, but they are not. They must be searching on foot." Stepping down out of the Jeep, Sarah walked over to the middle of the field, with her hands cupped around her mouth, forming a mini megaphone to project her voice she began to yell, "Chief, Chief, can you hear me? Chief, are you out there?"

She waited a few moments, then repeated, "Chief Order. Chief! Chief Order."

Sarah walked back to the Jeep where Whiskey was anxiously waiting and wanting to exit the Jeep. "What is it boy?"

Whiskey gave a little whimper, one that Sarah was very familiar with. "Oh, Whiskey, I am, sorry. In all the commotion, you haven't used the bathroom in hours."

Sarah opened the door. Whiskey jumped out, beelined to the front passenger side of the cruiser, lifted his leg and peed for a solid thirty seconds on the chief's front right tire.

"Are you kidding me, Whisk? I thought you liked the chief."

Laughing, Emily said, "Maybe he's trying to send a message to Arminius."

Smirking and looking back at Emily, Sarah said, "Whiskey was here!" I wonder if he was a graffiti artist, what would his tag be? A yellow stream?"

Scrunching her nose, Emily said, "Eww, sick! You weirdo!"

Whiskey jumped back into the Jeep. Sarah pushed the clutch in and started the ignition and slid the gear shifter into reverse. "Let's go find Mrs. Jenkins, Whiskey."

Whiskey acknowledged that his name was mentioned by licking Sarah's ear.

As the Jeep was pulling away, Fritz and Arminius emerged from the woods at the opposite end of the field, followed closely Chief Order and Agent Miles.

"Hey Chief, when Arminius and I stepped out of the woods, there was an old green Jeep pulling away."

"Old green Jeep. What color of green?"

Fritz said, "I'm not sure in English what it would be. It was rich in color, like maybe a four-leaf clover?"

Agent Miles looked at the chief. "Maybe a kelly green, since a four-leaf clover is Irish?"

"Fritz, if that was an old kelly-green Jeep, then that was Sarah. There are a lot of people that have Jeeps in Cottageville, but there is only one old kelly green one, and that's Sarah's."

Pulling out his cell phone from his back right pocket, the chief was about to call Sarah, when he realized he did not have service.

"Do either of you have phone service?" asked the chief.

Fritz and Agent Miles both confirmed that they did not.

"What would you like me to say, Chief? I can talk to the rest of the agents on our coms."

"Could you tell the rest of the team that we do not have cell service and are going to continue to travel up the dirt road and that we will maintain contact with everyone via coms."

As the chief, Fritz, and Arminius made their way back to the cruiser, Agent Miles walked a few steps behind, talking on his com.

Opening the back passenger side door and sliding in, Agent Miles directed his question to the chief. "Why would Sarah be up here?"

"That's like asking a small child, why did you eat the cookie when I told you not to? All I can say is, I know Sarah, and she didn't hear you are no longer allowed to be involved with this case. She heard, this is official business, so you cannot travel with the FBI."

"Oh, a tenacious female, ah!"

"She's spunky for sure, but she's got a great heart and would do just about anything for anyone. Including risking her life to save Mrs. Jenkins."

Turning his head toward both the Chief and Agent Miles, Fritz said, "That's concerning at this present moment. We need to catch up to her."

"I agree, Fritz. And I am surprised that I sense compassion in your voice, I thought Germans were stoic and a bit cold."

"*Ihr Amerikaner,* why is it you think you understand other cultures so well?"

Regretting his comment, the chief responded, "Easy, Fritz, I was just messing with you."

"*Sicher warst du das,*" said Fritz.

"What? I didn't catch that." Chief Order smiled at Fritz.

The police cruiser sped as fast as the dirt road would allow to try to close the distance between them and Sarah, but they lagged about a mile.

Sarah, Emily, and Whiskey were getting closer to Bunky's abandoned place.

"How do you know where you are going?" asked Emily.

"Occasionally Whiskey and I drive up here. I care too much for my Jeep, so I don't take it four wheeling, but this dirt road is off the beaten path enough to still feel like I am four wheeling without the risk of damaging my girl."

"It is nice up here," responded Emily.

"If I am not mistaken, we will make another steep climb, go through a series of sharp curves, then we will see Bunky's driveway on the left. I don't know how far down the driveway goes though, because you can't see the house from the road."

"Sarah, what are we going to do when we get there?"

"We will park and see if we have cell signal again. If not, we will sneak down the driveway to the house."

With a look of panic on her face, Emily said, "Sarah, this sounds dangerous! Are you sure?"

"Just think of Mrs. Jenkins. That poor woman has been missing for days. She needs our help."

"I know, it's just, I am only a sophomore in college, I am too young to die."

Not sure if Emily was serious or playing, Sarah only said, "Everything will be fine."

After the Jeep made the steep climb and passed through a series of tight turns, they slowly approached the driveway, and it was just like Sarah described it. The entrance was on the left side of the road, the driveway was long, and no house was visible from the road.

They noticed an old white mailbox smashed and lying beside the driveway's entrance and Sarah didn't think that was a good sign. But she ventured on. Sarah pulled off the dirt road and parked in a flat patch of tall weeds and switchgrass. She opened her door and jumped out of the Jeep. "Let's go, Whiskey. Let's find Mrs. Jenkins."

"Sarah, we still don't have cell signal."

"Well, hopefully Ginger and Jared received your text message, and they know where we are if something happens."

Emily mumbled, "Wow. That's comforting."

Crouching low, Sarah was in full-fledged action hero mode.

"Let's cut down through the woods and try to stay behind the tree lines, that way they won't see us coming. Come on, Whiskey."

Whiskey crouched and gracefully glided closer to the ground. Meanwhile, Emily continued to voice her concerns.

"Em, you gotta shut up!" Sarah pleaded.

"But ..."

Interrupting Emily, Sarah turned around and glared at her. "Shh. If you can't handle it, go lock yourself in the Jeep."

Emily's eyes widened and Sarah saw fear. Then Emily ran her hand in front of her mouth zipping her lips and throwing away the key. The trio proceeded with caution, descending the hill with wary steps. Though they were still at a considerable distance, their eyes caught sight of an eerie white van stationed on the left side of the house.

"Ewww, that's a major creeper van," Emily whispered.

"Yeah, I see it. From here, it looks like it doesn't have a license plate either."

"This is like a movie scene that went terrible bad for a teenaged girl."

"That's a movie. This is real life. We got this, Em."

Whiskey's ears perked up as he gave a little growl and lowered his belly all the way to the ground, like child using the army crawl to move forward.

"What is it, Whisk?" asked Sarah.

"Sarah, get down." Sarah felt Emily's hand on her shoulder pushing her down as Emily squatted behind a large oak tree.

"I see him now too. Thank you for the warning," said Sarah.

Determined to remain hidden, they hunkered down as close

to the ground as possible. Their focus fixated on an overweight man wearing ripped blue jeans, a white t-shirt, and a camouflage jacket. With long, matted hair that brushed his shoulders, he busily shuffled items in the van through the sliding side door.

About ten minutes passed before the man slid the side door of the van shut and disappeared back into the old house.

"You ready? Let's work our way up to the side of the van," Sarah suggested.

"Ready? No. But does that matter?"

Similar to well-trained soldiers, they maneuvered around a mound of dirt and navigated through a thorny patch of briars without making a sound. They positioned themselves on the side of the van that faced away from the house, ensuring they remained hidden from view.

"Stay here with Whiskey, Emily, I am going to sneak around to the back of the house and try looking in through one of the windows."

Without giving Emily a second to respond, Sarah was gone. Emily laid flat on her belly under the van and watched Sarah's feet as they disappeared around the corner of the house.

"Whiskey, what are we doing here?"

Whiskey scooted up closer to Emily and nudged her with his cold, wet nose.

"Thanks, boy. You are such an encourager."

Suddenly, the side door of the house was thrown open and Emily and Whiskey were now staring at old work boots, as the heavy man was back at the open van door.

Huddled beneath the van, Emily found herself silently mouthing fragments of the Lord's Prayer.

"Lead us not into temptation, but ...."

As the word "but" left Emily's soundless lips, the man dropped a can of beer, which rolled under the van. In a loud raspy voice, he grumbled, "Stupid can of beer!"

He got down onto his knees, and he mumbled, "Where did you go?" And he peered under the van. He not only found his dropped can of beer, but he also found Emily and Whiskey lying down in the dirt driveway.

"What the, where did you come from?" said the large man as he reached under the van toward Emily.

With a sudden burst of aggression, Whiskey lunged forward, his jaws snapping shut on the man's forearm, his teeth sinking into the flesh with a firm grip.

Emily quickly scrambled out from under the van and sprinted away. She shouted, "Run, Whiskey, run." Emily took off up the driveway, back toward the road.

Whiskey was tenacious. The man's attempt to disengage only fueled Whiskey's determination, as the canine tightened his hold even more. The scene resembled a tumultuous contest of strength, like a fierce tug of war, except the man's arm served as the substitute for the rope.

With pain and desperation seeping into his voice, the large man cried out to his comrade inside the house, pleading for help. "John! John, help me! John!"

As the man's plea dissipated into the surrounding forest, Whiskey was determined to hold him pinned under the van.

The side door of the house slapped open, and John exited. He saw his friend sprawled out face down, with half his body under the van. "What the crap you doing?"

"Help me. There is a dog ripping my arm apart. It won't let go."

John crouched down on his hands and knees to get a look. "Dumb dog, where did you come from?"

John stood again and began to circle to the other side of the van. Aware of John's location, Whiskey slid forward under the van and turned his body away from John, while keeping a firm jaw on the big man's forearm.

"Come on. Get this dog off of me." He tried to push Whiskey's head with his free hand.

"Hold on, Ralph. I am going to find a stick and beat him to death."

After scouring the woods, John emerged, clutching a hefty branch in his hands, as he made his way toward the van.

Crying from the pain, Ralph was begging Whiskey to let go.

As John approached the van, he told Ralph he'd be free in a moment. Leaning forward and peering under the van, John looked at Whiskey. "You are going to die, dog."

CHAPTER TWENTY-TWO

Sarah managed to sneak into the house. Cautiously, she searched. With each step, she treaded lightly, her heart pounding in her chest. She discreetly explored each room of the abandoned old house.

Sarah could hear the yelling and commotion outside, which made her even more anxious. *Come on, Mrs. Jenkins. I know you are here.*

Turning down the dark south hallway of the old house, Sarah turned the doorknob to the first room on the right and slowly pushed the creaky door open.

"Oh my God, Mrs. Jenkins!"

Sarah rushed over to Mrs. Jenkins, who had her mouth taped

shut and was duct taped to an old wooden kitchen chair. She wore filthy and torn flannel pajamas.

Pulling her trusted pocketknife that Uncle Tom gave her out of her front left pocket, Sarah cut Mrs. Jenkins free and took the tape from her mouth, apologizing the whole time for causing her pain and removing a layer of her skin.

Desperate to get out of the house, Sarah asked, "Can you walk, Mrs. Jenkins?"

"Sarah, these old bones are ready to run!"

Smiling at the woman's wit, "Let's run then!"

Sarah and Mrs. Jenkins ran out the back door of the house and went around the opposite side of the house from where the van was parked. They paused for a moment, making sure it was clear for them to move up the hill, back to the road.

Just as they were making a move forward, Sarah heard Whiskey's shrill cry. *What?* Sarah thought. *He's in pain.*

Now frozen in contemplation, Sarah stood still. *Do I save my boy, or do I take Mrs. Jenkins up to the road?*

John and Ralph yelled at each other and at Whiskey. "Hit him again. The dumb animal won't let me go."

Sarah's heart dropped. She had a mental image of her Whiskey being beaten by some big evil man. *I've gotta do something,* she thought.

Sarah told Mrs. Jenkins to run straight up the hill through the woods and not to stop until she came to the dirt road. "I can't let them kill my dog."

Before Mrs. Jenkins could respond, Sarah was already darting around the corner of the house but was abruptly halted by the loud sound of a gunshot. Sarah dove to the ground and crawled close to the house. She carefully peeked around the corner toward the van.

The front windshield of the van had exploded, and the two men went running. Sarah saw Whiskey beelining for her.

"Thank God," she said, as she flipped over onto her back and looked up toward the sky for a moment before standing to her feet. Before Sarah turned the corner of the old house, Whiskey was there jumping on her, with a bloody mouth and injured leg, but happy as ever to see his favorite human.

Stooping down and reaching her arms around Whiskey's neck, Sarah reminded Whiskey how much she loved him. She looked at his mouth and realized it was fine. The blood wasn't his.

With his government issued M4 carbine drawn, Agent Miles followed Whiskey to Sarah. "You okay, miss?"

"Yes, but you might want to check on Mrs. Jenkins. She's around the side of the house."

Agent Miles headed in that direction and was followed by Sarah and Whiskey. They found Mrs. Jenkins down behind an overgrown Rhododendron.

"It's okay, ma'am, you can come out now. You are safe," Agent Miles said.

Peeking up over the bush, Mrs. Jenkins slowly stood to her feet and made her way toward the agent.

As Whiskey, Sarah, Agent Miles, and Mrs. Jenkins walked toward the white creeper van, the Black SUV carrying Director Mason and the rest of the agents came barreling down the driveway.

"The cavalry has arrived," joked Agent Miles.

Chief Order had John cuffed with his hands behind his back, sitting on the ground against the front passenger tire of the white van. Fritz had Ralph face down on the dirt driveway, with his left hand behind his back and his right, bleeding arm extended up over his head, while Fritz leaned his left knee into his back to hold him on the ground.

The agents piled out of the SUV with guns drawn and made their way around the perimeter of the house. In a swift and coordinated manner, they entered the premises, executing a rapid search of the entire house. Satisfied that there were no threats, they promptly retreated to the white van.

"All clear, Director," said Agent Fox.

Director Mason turned toward Chief Order. "Can we put these two in the back of the cruiser and take them to the station?"

"Absolutely, Director. It would be my pleasure to lock these two up."

The agents watched over John and Ralph, while Fritz retreated and conversed with Director Mason. Chief Order walked up the long driveway to retrieve the cruiser.

When the chief arrived back at the house, Emily and Arminius jumped out of the car. "OMG, Sarah, I am so glad you are okay."

Arminius went straight to Whiskey and licked his face and nudged his neck. He curled next to him, and it was clear to Sarah Arminius was trying to provide comfort. "You're a great friend," Sarah said.

Five minutes later the caravan was on the dirt road headed toward Route Nine. The criminals were secured in the back of the cruiser with Arminius riding in the front, in between the chief and

Fritz. Mrs. Jenkins accompanied Director Mason and the other agents in the black SUV, and Agent Miles and Agent Fox rode with Sarah, Emily, and Whiskey in the back seat of the 1969 CJ5.

Agent Miles removed a packet of hand sanitizer wipes from a pouch in his vest and gently cleaned the blood on Whiskey's snout and leg. "Sorry, buddy. This might sting."

Whiskey let out a little whimper, but it appeared more from his leg pain than from the alcohol in the wipes.

"Whiskey's leg looks bad. It might be a good idea to have it x-rayed."

"My poor guy," said Sarah. "I'll take a look at it when we get back to town."

The three-vehicle caravan quickly passed through town and arrived at the police station. Agents Miles and Fox departed from the Jeep and entered the station. Sarah and Emily knew they didn't have a place at the station, so they drove to the Coiffure to exam Whiskey's injuries.

"What a crazy day, Emily."

"Crazy day? How about a crazy few days?"

"Crazy days for sure, but even crazier is that we solved the case. Can you believe it?"

Emily stood up straight and puffed up her chest. "And we didn't even need the FBI!"

"No, we didn't, but it sure was nice to have Chief James and Fritz show up when they did."

"When that guy tried to grab me, Whiskey saved me. He lunged at the guy's arm and would not let it go. That gave me time to crawl out backwards from under the van, then I ran as fast as I could up the hill toward the road. I'm sorry, but I never even looked back. I was in fight or flight mode. But I don't know how to fight, so I chose flight. I am sorry, Sarah, that I ran away."

Looking over at Emily, Sarah said, "Don't be ridiculous, you did the right thing. You could have gotten hurt if you hadn't run."

"But Whiskey got hurt instead. And what about you? I didn't even know where you went."

"Emily, it's all right. Everything worked out and we saved Mrs. Jenkins."

Pulling up in front of the Coiffure, Sarah asked Emily if she could unlock the front door while she got Whiskey out of the Jeep.

"Come here, boy." Sarah slid her hands under Whiskey's belly and pulled him against her chest. "Why do you seem heavier today, huh, Whiskey?"

Sarah carried Whiskey into the Coiffure and placed him gently on one of the grooming tables. Emily prepared gauze pads and handed them to Sarah to clean Whiskey's wounds. After attending to the cuts on his snout, forehead, and neck, Sarah began examining Whiskey's leg.

"Feel this, Emily. What do you think?"

"It's definitely swollen, but I do not feel a break."

"Yeah, that's what I think too, but what if it's fractured and we can't feel it?"

"Good point. Do you want me to call Dr. Schank and schedule an x-ray for Whiskey?"

"Let's hold off until tomorrow, Em. I will give him some pain meds and keep an eye on him tonight and see how he is in the morning."

"Okay. What do we do now?"

"What do you mean, Emily?"

"Are we supposed to go home and act like nothing happened? Aren't you dying to know who the guys are that abducted Mrs. Jenkins?"

"Oh, Emily, even though I'm concerned for Whiskey, I can't stop thinking about it. We should be there at the station with the official-business-only people!"

"Yes, we should, and besides, Mrs. Jenkins needs some other females to support her. I am sure she is suffering being around all those hot agents in uniform."

"Emily, you crack me up. Since when does my emo assistant have a thing for older guys in a uniform?"

"Since your emo assistant got to be around hot federal agents in uniforms!"

Sarah carried Whiskey to his plush memory foam bed on the floor of the waiting area. She bent down and kissed Whiskey's forehead. "You be a good boy and get some rest. Emily and I will be back in a little bit."

"Come on, Em, let's go back to the station and get some answers."

"Wait, Sarah, I thought we were going for some hot federal agents," said Emily.

Laughing, Sarah responded, "I thought you had two hot Ts already. Could you really handle a few special agents too?"

"I guess I will have to try and find out."

Emily and Sarah hopped into the Kelly Green Jeep and turned down Second Street toward the station. Looking down at her black platform Vans, Emily said, "Dang it, I knew they were going to get dirty."

Chuckling, Sarah said, "At least you are alive to talk about it!"

Emily looked up from her shoes and over toward Sarah. "Point taken!"

"I would be glad to buy you two pairs of platform Vans in any color you want. I'm just glad everyone is okay and that we saved Mrs. Jenkins."

"Thanks, Sarah, but I am sure I can clean these. And I'm glad the case has been solved too."

As they approached the police station, they noticed the Black SUVs parked in a single file line in front of the station, with all the agents posted in strategic spots around the perimeter of the building.

"Sarah, what's going on? I thought the bad guys were captured today."

"I am sure it's just protocol. Let's park around back and see if we are allowed in."

Finding a spot in an open lot behind the station, Sarah parked between a silver lifted Dodge Ram 2500 and a new black Tesla. She was always selective about where she parked, not wanting door dings on her classic ride.

"I read in a spy novel once that if you act like you know what you are doing and walk with confidence, you can get into places you shouldn't have access to. Let's walk straight past the agents and in through the front door like we own the place."

"You crack me up, Sarah. How about I just follow your lead on this on."

Turning the corner of the building and walking down the sidewalk toward the front door of the station, Sarah greeted the agents, "Gentlemen, good to see you again." She mumbled under her breath, "Just smile and keep walking, Emily."

Arriving at the front door, Sarah puffed her chest out and held her head high, "Agents, we are here to see Chief Order," Sarah said with determination in her voice.

"Yes, ma'am," replied Agent Lee. "Chief Order informed us that you'd be coming."

Walking past the agents and into the police station, Sarah turned to Emily, "Did Agent Lee say the chief was expecting us?"

"Well not us, but you, Sarah."

Before Sarah could respond, Chief Order was calling for her. "Sarah. Sarah. Emily. Can you two come with me please?"

Surprised, Sarah said, "Sure, Chief, "What's up?"

Chief Order ushered Emily and Sarah down the hall to a conference room where Mrs. Jenkins was being attended to by Walter and Wendy Parks, Cottageville's volunteer medics.

Lighting up like a tree on Christmas day, Mrs. Jenkins directed a huge, heartfelt smile towards Sarah and Emily. "You two are amazing humans. From what I've been told, if it weren't for you, I wouldn't have been rescued from those thugs!"

Reaching down to wrap her arms around Mrs. Jenkins, Sarah held her and, in a soft gentle voice, told her, "I'm glad you are safe, and I think you are one of the good guys."

Mrs. Jenkins pulled back and looked startled. "What does that mean?"

Sarah looked into Mrs. Jenkin's warm eyes. "Nothing, Mrs. Jenkins. I will explain another time."

"How is she, Wendy?" Sarah inquired.

"She's dehydrated and has minor cuts and bruises, but other than that, she's in great health."

"Awesome," replied Sarah.

Emily now leaned over into Mrs. Jenkins and gave her a side hug. "Welcome back, Mrs. Jenkins."

"Thank you, Emily, it's good to be back. Though I like the woods, that wasn't my idea of a good time." Mrs. Jenkins grinned. "How did you do it, Sarah? How did you know something happened to me?"

"It was Whiskey, Mrs. Jenkins. He's the one that knew something was wrong. We were coming home after work, and he went up onto your porch and to your front door. I kept calling him and tried to get him to leave, but he was insistent. He nudged your door and sat down on your mat. After much coaxing, I finally was able to get him home. The next morning, when we were leaving the house for work, he went straight to your door again, like a fox hound tracking a kit. I followed him up the stairs to your front porch and noticed what looked like blood on the railing. Then I saw sticks with sheared off ends poking up in the middle of the azalea bush, some little broken branches, and crushed pink petals. Honestly, I wasn't sure what to think at that point. I thought maybe you fell in the garden and cut yourself, and as you climbed up the stairs, you got your blood on the railing. I was concerned, but it was so early I didn't want to disturb you. Whiskey was acting erratic, pacing back and forth and sniffing the front door and stairs. Then, as if he was hot on a raccoon trail, Whiskey went down the stairs, through the flower beds and around back. I turned, went down the stairs, and followed close behind him. When I made it to the backyard, Whiskey was on the first step of your cement stoop barking toward the back door. The screen door was hanging off its hinges and the back door was ajar. That's when I decided to call Chief James."

"Oh, my goodness, Sarah. I wonder what day that was," said Mrs. Jenkins. "I was just turning in for the night and went to check the locks when the door flew open, and I was grabbed from behind and thrown to ground. I was so startled that I was dazed for a moment. When I realized what had just happened, the big, long-haired guy reached down and grabbed my hair to pull me to my feet. As he was pulling me up, I guess old instincts kicked in and I kicked out at him and hit the guy I learned later was named Ralph square on the side of the head. He looked like he had been just hit by Mike Tyson and not an old lady, because he stumbled backwards and let go of my hair. What I did next not only shocked him but shocked me as well. I took one step backwards, pulled my right knee high, and extended out my leg like I was kicking a door down. I hit that guy in the middle of his chest with the perfect push kick and sent him backwards off the porch into my flower bed below. I immediately pushed my front door open, got into the house, and locked the door."

Emily asked, "Weren't you scared?"

"Not at that moment, Emily. I didn't feel anything, I only knew

I was going to do what it took to survive."

"I would have been scared stiff," Sarah added.

Wendy Parks spoke up that she would have been crying like a baby for a bottle.

Wendy's husband, Walter, laughed. "She's not kidding. Wendy shuts down when she'd scared."

"I get that, but for me with all my years of training and assignments, I have learned to control my reactions. As beneficial as our fight or flight response is, as an agent, it can get you killed. I have learned to not react to certain stimuli, to keep my mind-body connection working well and not be overcome with emotions."

"Wow, Mrs. Jenkins, that's crazy," responded Emily.

"Keep going, tell us what happened next," Sarah prompted.

Mrs. Jenkins continued her story. "I debated calling nine-one-one, but decided I had enough time to get upstairs, get my Glock out of the gun safe, and lock myself in the bathroom before I made the call. What I didn't realize though, was that John was already kicking in the back door. I saw Ralph through the glass on the front door, but never thought about there being an accomplice entering through the back. John splintered the back door open and chased me half-way up the staircase, before grabbing my left leg and pulling me down hard on the stairs. That was it, I had no fight left in me. I figured it was better to cooperate."

Hanging on to Mrs. Jenkins' every word, Sarah said, "I can literally visualize all of this while you speak. Now it makes sense. The broken azalea bush and crushed pink flowers were from Ralph's big body when he crashed to the ground after you kicked him off the porch. The blood on the railing must have been his, but I all this time I assumed it was yours."

There was a knock on the door, and Director Mason entered the room and pulled up a chair on the opposite side of the meeting room table from Mrs. Jenkins. "How are you feeling, June?"

Sarah thought it was odd hearing Mrs. Jenkins be called June, because they all knew her as Janice.

"I'm fine, Director Mason." She pointed to the Parks. "These two say I am dehydrated and have some abrasions and bruises, but I think they would say I am fine as well."

The Parks nodded their heads, agreeing with Mrs. Jenkins' assessment.

"You know, Director, if they wouldn't have had the jump on me, I think I could have taken them."

He smiled from ear to ear and leaned back in his chair. "I bet you could have. I bet you could have."

"Director, would you be so kind to allow me to finish telling the story to my wonderful friends before you take me to Washington?"

Sarah frowned.

"Yes, Sarah, we had this conversation before," responded Director Mason.

"Sarah, it's okay. I have broken a lot of laws and am tired of covering my tracks. Plus, I can't erase my footprints anymore, as is evident from this whole ordeal."

"Why, what changed? You've remained hidden for all these years," said Sarah.

"My longtime friend, Special Agent Trout, was my inside guy

erasing my existence everywhere I went. He and my husband were close friends, so he was determined to help me avenge his death and keep me safe. Unfortunately, he suffered a massive heart attack three weeks ago and died at the Quantico Clinic. Obviously, no one knew that he was in contact with me, so I was never notified of his death. With his passing, I lost my covering, and my footprints began to surface. Somehow, someone recognized my aliases, and the dark web chatter began."

Director Mason shook his head. "Agent Trout! I would have never guessed it!"

"Yes. Like I said, we go way back."

The Parks said they had to go because they had a call from dispatch. Mrs. Watson needed an ambulance to take her to the hospital because she suffered from chest pain and shortness of breath.

Everyone said their thank yous and goodbyes to the Parks as they exited the conference room and headed down the hall.

"Get back to the story, Mrs. Jenkins," encouraged Emily.

"Okay, so those thugs dragged me out of my house and put me in a white van. I had no idea what had happened. I figured I would be picked off one day from a mile away by a sniper, not abducted by street thugs. Honestly, I didn't know what they wanted, and they seemed confused themselves. The big guy drove the van, but the other one seemed to be the boss. Well, I thought he was until we arrived at that house up in the woods. When we arrived, there was a third man there waiting for us. He was the head of the operation. I say operation, but it was not an operation like we know it, Director Mason. These guys were clueless."

Intrigued, Sarah asked who the third person was.

"I heard them call him Carson, and I learned he is Bunky Buffalo's cousin. That's how they knew about the abandoned house. Carson is a hacker and buys and sells codes, crypto, and other random things on the dark web. He was the one that heard about my identity and devised a plan to hold me for ransom and sell me out to others that might come looking for me."

"Where is Carson now?" asked the Director. "We only found Ralph and John at the house."

"He left. I think he said he was going to hide out at a friend's house in Miami. Carson isn't a violent person. He's very intelligent and uses his brain to make money. Granted, his business might not be legal, but he has no intention of hurting people. He saw me as a quick way to make a buck, but needed help, so he hired the two thugs off the dark web. Honestly, I think he realized he was in over his head, once we got talking and he saw Ralph and John's instability."

Curious, Sarah asked, "So none of these guys actually knew who you really are or that you had all of the stolen jewelry?"

"That's the thing. Apparently, the intel was that I, a notorious thief and ex-special agent, was living a secret life in Cottageville and that there was a price on my head. The price on my head intrigued Carson, so much that he devised a plan to take an old woman hostage and wait for the person willing to pay the highest price."

"Why didn't Carson stay and wait for someone to come and pay?" Emily asked.

"You must understand, I only would hear bits and pieces of the conversations and telephone calls, but from what I could tell, the black web chatter picked up and people started threatening Carson when he offered my whereabouts for a price. You have to remember, the people looking for me are not amateurs playing games, they are highly trained and skilled professionals. Carson and the two goons, on the other hand, are the furthest thing from professionals. Like I said, Carson is smart. He knew he was going to get killed, so he wanted out. However, the two thugs he hired wouldn't back down and started threatening Carson, even though he hired them. That's when he left. But before he left, he apologized to me and said he was posting messages on the web. He hoped those things would help lead to my freedom."

"It was this Carson fellow that was posting messages in the Cottageville social feed," said Sarah.

Emily's enthusiasm was infectious. "Yeah, if it weren't for his messages, we would have never been able to find you."

"He may have posted on the message board because he was trying to ease his guilty conscience," said the director.

"I have no idea what the messages were or why he did them, all I know is that I am alive and grateful that it was thugs who abducted me and not people from my past."

"Understood," replied Director Mason.

There was a knock at the door, then it cracked open and Chief Order's face appeared. "May I come in?"

In unison, everyone agreed.

"Officer Beams and Officer Grimes interrogated John and Ralph and have received their confessions. They actually admitted to everything and gave a general timeline of events, which we will need to review with Mrs. Jenkins. They also informed the officers that there was a third accomplice, Carson Everett, who is Bunky Buffalo's cousin."

"That is correct, Chief James. Carson was the brains of the operation, but he bailed when things got hot and took off to Florida," said Mrs. Jenkins.

"Chief, he was the one that was posting the clues in the Cottageville social group. Without his help, we might not have located Mrs. Jenkins," Emily said. "We figure he also did the spray painting of June, though we aren't sure why."

"That's quite interesting. Why would he abduct Mrs. Jenkins then give hints on how to free her? As for the water tower, we all used that as a hang out when we were kids. Maybe he thought enough of Cottageville wasn't online, that old-school methods were also needed." He shrugged.

Looking over at him, Mrs. Jenkins said, "Sometimes when people do bad things, they aren't necessarily bad people."

Sarah busted out a laugh, "I cheer for the bad guys all the time!"

The room's heaviness immediately lifted, and their laughter could be heard down the hall in the reception area.

"Emily and Sarah, I appreciate all your help on this case. You have done a great job." The Director smiled. "You are true professionals in your amateur sleuth ways."

Once again, the room filled with laughter and Sarah thought, *I love my life in Cottageville and the community I have around me.*

Director Mason stood to his feet and turned to Emily and Sarah. "I am going to have to ask you two to leave, so Chief Order, Fritz, and I can meet with Mrs. Jenkins."

"Okay, sir, we understand," Sarah said.

She and Emily stood up, gave Mrs. Jenkins another hug, grinned at the chief, and exited the conference room into the hall.

Fritz passed them in the hallway and reminded them that they did an amazing job and that they should be proud.

Emily smiled and looked at Sarah. "Darn right, we did. Girl Power, baby. Right, Sarah?"

"That's right. Girl and cattle dog power!"

Emily giggled. "Don't tell Whiskey though that I said that, because without him, we wouldn't have even started on the case."

"It will be our secret."

Almost out of the police station, Emily said, "Sarah, I have two serious questions for you."

"Okay, what?"

Eyed her as they walked. "So, when do I get that raise you mentioned?"

Sarah chuckled. "It's effective immediately. You deserve it. What's your second question?"

With even a larger smile now plastered on her face, Emily asked, "When does the next mystery start?"

Sarah cracked up. "I have no idea. But let's go get Whiskey and take him home. He needs some time to heal before we stumble onto another adventure."

Paws and Puzzles

Want more Whiskey the Cattle Dog Mysteries? Read a sneak preview of book two in the series *Poodles and Poisons,* which will be released in spring 2024. To sign up to receive sneak previews and release dates about other books in the Whiskey Mystery Series, go to https://www.inyourfaceink.com/index.html

POODLES
AND
POISONS

CHAPTER 1

On a late August Sunday in Cottageville with the sun shining overhead and a light breeze swaying the trees, Sarah Carter, owner of Carter's Canine Coiffure, wore a purple halter dress in honor of Oodle the poodle's collar color as she stood in Gladys Rossmiller's backyard. Sarah's Australian red heeler cattle dog Whiskey stood alert and somber at her feet like a guard at Buckingham Palace.

Gladys was dressed in a black blouse and in black slacks, mirroring her grief. Tears trickled down her face as her neighbor and the owner of the local hardware store, Daniel Snyder, dug a hole between bushes in her rose garden. Thirty friends had gathered for the occasion of saying goodbye to Oodle and planting the urn with her ashes. No one knew exactly how old Oodle was when she went to her eternal sleep, but she and Gladys had been companions for more than two decades, and they belonged together the way Dalmatians did with firemen.

Sarah wiped a tear that slipped from her eye. Losing a beloved client was painful, and she and Whiskey, ever the empath, felt Gladys' grief like a tidal wave.

Wearing a black and white tweed suit—despite the summer heat—and sensible black shoes, Janice Jenkins, Sarah's next-door neighbor and Gladys' best friend, said a few words as the hole was dug. Janice was regaining her strength after surviving a kidnapping.

Chief James Order and his German shepherd Sascha were attending the service in Gladys' backyard. The chief held his hat over his heart and his eyes welled with unshed tears.

"Thank you all for gathering here today to remember Oodle," Janice said. "Oodle was a great poodle, and the perfect companion in Gladys' retirement, inspiring some of her best paintings."

The gathered friends smiled at that comment, and a few nodded their heads.

Janice continued, "Oodle was ever-present, loving, and a comfort to everyone, humans and other dogs alike. And we will miss her." She cleared her throat. "Would anyone like to share their favorite Oodle memory?" She looked around at all of the neighbors and their dogs, who were on their best behavior.

Daphne Smith, in a red maxi dress and a giant straw hat, held her French bulldog Pierre in one arm against her left side. She sniffed loudly before exclaiming, *"Je suis triste,"* and throwing the back of her right hand against her and flicking outward in a dramatic gesture

Sarah didn't understand.

"We all are," Sarah mumbled.

"*C'est horrible,*" Daphne added. She got sidelong looks from some people. Everyone in Cottageville knew or knew of Daphne and her penchant for everything French, though she was a town native and had never been to France.

"It is very sad," Janice agreed. "Does anyone else want to share?"

Robert Wise, who lived on Sarah's block and was the music teacher at the local high school, said he and his students had created a song to honor Oodle. He snapped three times and launched into a jazzy number about unconditional love; soft, curly fur; comfort; canine companionship; and dog being God spelled backwards. The number was both comedic and heart-breaking at the same time, and Sarah wasn't sure if she should laugh or cry, so she did a bit of both.

At one very moving part three-quarters of the way through, Gladys dabbed her face with a lace handkerchief, and Whiskey left Sarah's side to offer his soft fur to Gladys to stroke. Sarah's heart-space warmed as she watched Whiskey tap Gladys' leg twice with his front paw. Gladys leaned from her chair and hugged him like a child does a new puppy.

From across the circle of people, Emily Colt, the Coiffure's assistant groomer, spoke up. Her hair was dyed purple today in honor of Oodle, and she wore a short black dress, tights, and black combat boots. "I loved how gentle and trusting Oodle was. Even when her cataracts clouded her vision, she still trusted us to trim her nails and bathe her and showed us love and never feared. We could learn from her." Emily's voice cracked on the last few words.

Sarah sent her a weak, but appreciative smile and a nod of her head. "I loved how she romped with Whiskey, and even when Oodle was older and slower, he could still get her going and bring out her inner puppy. It was beautiful to see," Sarah said.

"Yes, it was," Gladys agreed. "They were so good together." She wiped another tear from her cheek and ruffled Whiskey's fur with her crooked and swollen knuckled fingers.

Whiskey wiggled closer to her in response, and Gladys chuckled.

Sarah's best friend and owner of Java and Juice, Ginger said, "As Oodle aged, I had to find a biscuit recipe that was softer than what I usually make for the dogs that come in. Because of her, I learned a lot about senior dog health and nutrition. I will miss hearing her nails click on our café floor. May you rest in peace, Oodle. You brought a lot of comfort and joy into our lives. And for that, we are grateful."

Sarah saw Daniel smile at Ginger. Sarah was the only one in town who knew Daniel and Ginger had gone on a couple of dates and were trying to figure out what they were to each other. Town gossip spread faster than the global pandemic in 2020 so they were keeping seeing each other on the downlow. Ginger had grown up in Cottageville and known Daniel and his late wife all of her life.

Bill, a widower who sat every morning on his front porch with a gallon jar of dog biscuits while he read the newspaper and drank his coffee, said that he would miss seeing Gladys and Oodle walk past his house daily. "She didn't have enough teeth to eat the biscuits I buy, so sometimes I'd soak one in some chicken broth for her."

Gladys said, "I'll still come by, Bill. But I'd prefer coffee to a soggy biscuit." That made her friends and neighbors laugh. Bill said, "Sure thing, Gladys."

Gladys smiled at him and then said, "I appreciate you all coming here today. I'm grateful for your love and support during this rough week. I know Oodle loved you all and I do, too. Daniel, if you'd be so kind to help this old lady..."

Daniel walked toward Gladys, but the chief got to her first. "Here, Gladys, I'll help you," Chief James said. He offered his elbow, and she put her arm through his.

He guided her across the lawn to the rose bushes, and Whiskey and Sascha followed them.

Daniel bent to the ground, picked up the urn, and held it toward Gladys.

She kissed the top of it and said, "Good dog." Tears ran rivulets down her cheeks. "I love you. Always." To Daniel she said, "I can't bend like I used to. Would you do the honors?"

In silence, Daniel crouched in front of the hole and placed the urn into it. Others in the yard crowded toward them, wanting to watch and to pay their final respects. Daniel scooped a hand spade of dirt and offered it to Gladys. The Chief walked her another foot closer to the edge of the hole. She tilted the spade and watched the soil stream over the urn.

"Thank you," Gladys said, handing the spade back to Daniel. Her tears had stopped, and her blue eyes were clear, though slightly bloodshot. Then she turned, everyone backed up a step or two to give her room, and the chief escorted her back to her chair. But instead of sitting, she said, "A luncheon is inside. Please help yourself. Chief, if you could accompany me into the kitchen. I need a cup of tea."

"My pleasure," Chief James said. He guided Gladys up the back steps onto the small deck and into her house. Janice, Bill, Daphne, and most of the others followed.

But Sarah, Ginger, Emily, Sascha, and Whiskey stayed outside while Daniel covered the urn and filled in the hole. The vet's office had made a plaster imprint of Oodle's paw, and Gladys had asked Daniel to use that as a grave marker amongst the roses. Daniel pushed it into the dirt half an inch to make it secure. Whiskey sniffed the plaster marker once and then walked a few feet away before lifting his leg on a bush. Sarah rolled her eyes and thought *At least he didn't mark the grave.*

"It's too bad Jared is away," Ginger said to Sarah. Ginger's blond curly hair framed her face instead of it being trapped in its usual ponytail or bun. Jared, Ginger's employee at the café, had been an integral part of Sarah's search for Mrs. Jenkins when she had disappeared. They had gone from having a joke-filled acquaintanceship to something more like a flirty friendship over the course of the summer. Sarah thought he would have appreciated the memorial service for Oodle, both for its quirkiness and because it brought a lot of the community together. Though Jared worked for Ginger at Java and Juice, his *real* vocation was writing and illustrating comic books and graphic novels, the latter of which he was shopping around to publishers. He was disappointed to miss the *Oodle fooneral*, as he called it, but he was in Vegas participating in Comic-Con. Over the last two days he had texted Sarah photos of people in all kinds of crazy costumes.

As Daniel and Ginger and Emily walked toward the back door

of Gladys' house, Sarah whistled for Whiskey and Sascha to come. They had been sniffing the newly dug grave and then every bush on both sides of the marker.

The dogs raced past her as she said, "Slow down." They stopped on the deck and waited for her to catch up. And then they walked like the perfect gentle dogs they were into Gladys' house, before slurping up water from a bowl in her kitchen.

Sarah small talked with people she knew, and she ate a cream cheese and cucumber finger sandwich and some potato salad. She cleared plates and cups and carried them from the living room and dining room into the kitchen. She was determined not to leave Gladys with a mess to clean up.

As she handwashed some china, Ginger popped into the kitchen and picked up a dishtowel to dry what Sarah was washing. "Did Daniel leave?" Sarah asked.

"He had to go back to the store." Daniel had inherited Buck and Son from his father. They were the only hardware store in town and were open seven days a week. Ginger carefully dried the bowl Sarah handed her. "Do you know where this goes?"

"I believe it belongs in the breakfront in the dining room." Sarah picked up a plate from the counter and dunked it in the wash water.

Ginger left the room with the bowl. When she returned, she said, "Whiskey is curled up in a corner of the dining room. Almost everyone has left. Gladys and Janice are sitting on a sofa together talking. I'll start to bring the food in. Can you find some smaller containers?"

"Sure. Just let me finish this plate."

Twenty minutes later, Sarah and Ginger had all of the leftover food in smaller containers and stacked in Gladys' refrigerator. They had washed and dried all the casserole dishes and cake and sandwich stands and left them on the kitchen table since they weren't sure where they went. But the rest of the kitchen and the dining room were clean.

"Thank you," Sarah said.

"Of course." Ginger smiled. "It's what best friends do."

"What are you up to the rest of the afternoon?" Sarah ran her hand through her ginger curls to push them out of her face.

"Daniel's coming over for dinner."

"Ooo la la," Sarah teased.

"It's going well, but we are taking it one date at a time."

"I don't see why," Sarah said. "You're both adults and know what you want. And that's not to be alone anymore. Makes sense to me." She winked at Ginger and then added, "Plus, he's a hard hunk of man. Why wouldn't you want that?"

Ginger laughed.

But Sarah understood, not wanting to be alone. She had been for quite a while—moving to Cottageville from Seattle by herself more than six years ago and inheriting her grandmother's house. Sarah felt less alone since Whiskey had come into her life, but it wasn't the same as having a human partner.

Sarah wondered how long Gladys would wait before she went to the animal shelter and got another dog. Sarah knew the silence of losing a pet and living alone could be too loud.

CHAPTER 2

Later in the week as Sarah and Whiskey made their rounds around town during their morning walk before work, they found Gladys sitting next to Bill on his front porch. The newspaper was spread in front of him on the table, but they appeared deep in conversation.

Sarah didn't want to interrupt, so she waved her hand in greeting. But Whiskey climbed Bill's stairs and parked his butt next to Bill's chair, waiting for his treat.

"Whiskey, Sarah, so glad to see you this morning," Gladys said. "Sarah, I was going to stop by later, but since I see you now... well...would you accompany me to the poodle rescue tomorrow after you close the Coiffure for the day?"

"I'd be honored. Does that mean you want another companion?"

Gladys' eyes looked large and shiny behind her glasses. "Yes, dear. I know it is soon, but I'm not getting any younger and I don't like that I now find myself talking to myself." Gladys grinned. "At least with a dog around I can talk to him or her and don't look batty."

Bill cracked up at the comment. "It's as good a reason as any to get another dog." He reached into his big glass jar and pulled out a beef dog biscuit, asked Whiskey for his paw, and then gave the dog the biscuit after they shook for it.

"I'd take Bill with me," Gladys said, "but you know more about dogs. And I know you and Whiskey will help me pick a good one."

"We will certainly try. Did you set a time with them?"

"Six o'clock. Is that okay?"

"It is. I will drive us. I'll swing by at 5:45 and pick you up."

"Thank you, dear." Gladys picked up her coffee mug and took a sip.

"My pleasure," Sarah said, waving for Whiskey to get off the porch and to come with her.

A few minutes later, Sarah pushed open the red door on Java and Juice which caused the bell above the door to jingle. Three people were in line in front of Jared, so Sarah eyed the pastry case noticing that the muffin of the day was banana walnut, the donuts were glazed, and the tarts were either lemon curd or raspberry. The case also contained the usual assortment of croissants, eclairs, and cinnamon and sugar-covered crullers. Her stomach rumbled like it demanded one of everything.

Sarah turned to walk to the end of the line and was surprised to find Whiskey already holding their place. "Smart dog," she said, rubbing his head between his ears. He knew he'd receive a homemade chicken biscuit as soon as it was his turn in front of Jared.

And sure enough, Jared smiled and said, "Whiskey, my man," and reached over the counter to five high Whiskey's right front paw. Then he tossed the biscuit into the air and Whiskey popped up to catch it with the enthusiasm of snagging a fly ball to win the World Series.

"Mi'lady," Jared said to Sarah, and he bowed from his waist in mock chivalry. "What can I get for her royal highness today?" He reached for her empty to-go coffee mug so it could be filled with their house blend black coffee.

"Two barbeque chicken salads, one each of the tarts, and a cruller, my lord." Sarah held her hands on the edges of an imaginary skirt and curtsied.

"A feast fit for a lady...or two." Jared's blue eyes sparkled.

Sarah ran her credit card through the machine on the counter, adding a healthy twenty-five percent tip for Jared, and then reached for her go-cup and the bag with her food. "I'm glad you are back," she said quietly.

"Me, too," Jared said. "I'll text you later."

"Sounds good."

Suddenly a thump came from a corner table and Sarah turned to see what had happened. A man she didn't know hit the table again with his fist as his face turned purple. From his throat came wheezes like a St. Bernard with emphysema.

"Call nine-one-one," Sarah said, racing toward the man's table, with Whiskey by her side.

"Are you choking?" she asked, putting her stuff on his table, before getting behind him to start the Heimlich maneuver. She pumped her fist into his stomach once and then again and again, but nothing came out and his wheezing got worse.

Ginger and Jared were both at the table now. "Choking or an allergy?" Ginger asked.

The man's eyes bugged like a pug's at Ginger's question.

She turned and looked around her café. "Anyone have an epi-pen?"

No one responded.

Within five minutes the front door pushed open, the bell tinkled, and Wendy and Walter Parks, the town's volunteer paramedics, rushed in carrying a bag of medical supplies and pushing a stretcher. They were followed by Officer John Beams.

The man's hands were now on his throat as he struggled to breathe. Wendy pulled out a liquid filled syringe and jammed the needle into the man's thigh. His whole body went rigid, and his eyes widened before he released an audible breath. The man noisily sucked air into his body before forcing it back out. In and out, in and out.

"Here, let's give you some oxygen to help elevate your saturation levels," Walter said. He pulled out a silicone oxygen mask that had hosing attached to a small tank.

"I'll be fine," the man rasped, shaking his head no.

"We have to take you in for an evaluation," Walter insisted. "All of that epinephrine can save your life, but the symptoms can return when it wears off."

The man, who Sarah guessed was in his fifties, gave Walter a hard stare.

"I'm serious," Walter said. "Plus, you may need additional treatment."

Wendy pushed the rolling bed closer to the table. "Hop on and we'll give you a free ride." She smiled at the man.

Officer Beams stepped forward and guided the man to standing with a hand on his elbow. The man said nothing but climbed aboard and Walter slipped the mask over his face.

Barbara Order, the chief's wife who had been sitting at a table by the door with her best friend, stood and opened the door for the Parks and the stretcher. Once they were safely outside and loading the man into the ambulance, Officer Beams said, "Anyone want to tell me what happened? Sarah? Ginger?" He pulled out a chair at the table, sat, and motioned for them to do the same. Jared walked back to his position at the register, and the rest of the café resumed what they had been doing before the drama.

Sarah said, "I didn't notice the man, really, until he pounded his hand on the table. Then I realized he was in trouble. But I thought he choked so I started the compressions on his diaphragm."

Ginger picked up, "But that wasn't working, and the man was gasping like a fish out of water and seemed to be getting worse. That's when I realized he could be having an allergic reaction, so I asked if anyone had an injector."

"And that's when Wendy and Walter came in. And you," Sarah finished.

Officer Beams had pulled a small tablet out of his pocket and made a few notes. "What did he purchase?" He looked at the table to muffin crumbs sticking to the paper wrapper and the empty cappuccino cup.

Ginger looked toward Jared and asked, "Muffin, cap, anything else?"

Jared said, "Cappuccino with hemp milk, banana walnut muffin, ham and cheese croissant sandwich. Oh, and he bought an orange."

Sarah, Ginger, and Officer Beams looked at the tabletop. There was no sign of orange. *Weird. Had he put it in his pocket?* Sarah stuck her head under the bistro table and looked at the wooden floor. *Had it fallen off when he banged the table?*

"Does anyone see an orange on the floor?" she asked over the din.

People glanced under their tables and around the room. But no one said, "I see an orange."

Jared held up an orange from a basket on the counter and called Whiskey. "Whiskey, see this? Go get it? Where it is, boy?" Whiskey ran to Jared and sniffed the orange that Jared held in front of his nose.

Whiskey thumped his red and white tail enthusiastically then zigged one way across the café and then the other sniffing here and sniffing there.

The café patrons encouraged him by patting his head as he came past or saying, "Good boy. Where it is?" Or "Go, Whiskey, find the orange."

He wiggled his nose along the baseboard of one wall all of the way to the bathroom door before jerking his head up, giving one sharp bark, and scratching the door with his paw.

Officer Beams got up and opened the bathroom door for

Whiskey and followed behind him. When they re-emerged, John had an orange in his hand, and the dog walked with the confidence of Beyonce at his side. "It was in the trash can. He went right to it."

The café erupted into claps. Sarah hugged her cattle dog, and Ginger gave him a second biscuit.

Officer Beams bagged the orange. "I'm not sure why this was in the trash, but since that seems suspicious and we still aren't sure what happened—"

"Or even who that man is," Sarah added.

John Beams smiled at her. "Yes, that too. I'm taking this with me." To Ginger he said, "I'll be back if I need more information."

"Of course," Ginger said, and then added more to herself than to anyone else, "Though I don't know why you'd order things you might be allergic to."

Officer Beams approached the counter. "Jared, did he ask about any ingredients in what he ordered?"

"No. Not at all. He asked if we had hemp milk, saying he preferred it or oat, but we ran out of oat milk earlier this morning."

"Okay. Well, while I'm here, can I get a black coffee to go?"

"Sure thing." Jared poured the coffee into a tall paper cup and eyed Ginger before saying, "It's on the house."

"Bribing an officer after poisoning someone, are you?" Officer Beams joked.

"I would never," Jared insisted, his grin flashing his top row of teeth.

Sarah and Whiskey left Java and Juice with Officer Beams. "What a way to start the day," Sarah said as they were walking down the sidewalk. "I hope that man will be okay."

"I'll follow up with him at the hospital. Thank you, Sarah, for your quick thinking on the Heimlich."

"Even if it wasn't necessary." Sarah smiled.

"You never know," John said. "Have a good day." He unlocked the cruiser parked at the curb.

Sarah and Whiskey walked two more blocks to Carter's Canine Coiffure, which had already been unlocked and set up for the day by Emily. Sarah set the breakfast food and her coffee on the counter and put their salads in the fridge in the back room of the converted house. Emily's purple hair had been teased into spikes and she wore a bone-patterned apron over a black rock concert t-shirt and jeans.

Sarah grabbed a cartoon corgi apron from a hook and tied it around her waist. "It's been quite a morning." She launched into the story about the man at the café.

"Have you seen him around here before?" Emily asked as Sergio's two shelties Sebastian and Sophie pranced through the door followed by Sergio himself. Whiskey greeted the shelties with a sniff and licked the ear of Sophie. "Here," Sergio said, thrusting the leashes at Sarah. "Barbara is blowing up my phone. I'm five minutes late for her color. But the kids didn't want to cooperate this morning. They were like oooh, we have to smell this and oooh, we have to smell that." He threw up his hands like he was over it.

Sarah laughed. "Dogs will be dogs. We'll have them ready by lunchtime. I saw Barbara this morning and I'm sure she hates that her roots are showing."

"You have no idea," Sergio said, before turning and trouncing through the door.

Emily laughed. "Cottageville drama. Now back to the man. So, you saved his life—"

"Probably Wendy did."

"But you have no idea who he is."

"Nope. He wore a white short-sleeve dress shirt and dress pants."

Emily cut in, "So he dressed like a Mormon on his mission?"

The remark surprised Sarah but when she thought for a split second, she realized that yes, the man was dressed as she had seen many Mormon missionaries dress. "Yes, though he was much older than mission age. I'd say mid-fifties."

"So, they took him away in the ambulance?"

"Yes. Apparently once you are injected with epinephrine you have to seek emergency medical care."

"Good to know," Emily said, starting the water and scooping up Sebastian. "I'll wash this one today and you wash Sophie."

"Okay. Oh, and Gladys asked me to go with her to look at rescue poodles tomorrow night. Isn't that sweet."

"Wow. Moving on already. Good for her."

Sarah started the water and put Sophie in the tub. Whiskey sat at her feet watching his friends get their baths and being groomed, until he was distracted by Officer John Beams walking through the Coiffure front door.

To never miss a Whiskey Mystery release, sign up here: https://www.inyourfaceink.com/index.html